Dead Girls

Don't Write Letters

Dead Girls Don't Write Letters

GAIL GILES

ROARING BROOK PRESS • BROOKFIELD, CONNECTICUT

Published by Roaring Brook Press
A Division of The Millbrook Press
2 Old New Milford Road
Brookfield, Connecticut 06804

LIBRARY OF CONGRESS CATALOGING-IN-PUBLICATION DATA

Giles, Gail.
   Dead girls don't write letters / Gail Giles.-- 1st ed.
   p. cm.
Summary: Fourteen-year-old Sunny is stunned when a total stranger shows
up at her house posing as her older sister Jazz, who supposedly died out
of town in a fire months earlier.
   [1. Sisters—Fiction. 2. Death—Fiction. 3. Mystery and detective
   stories.] I. Title.
   PZ7.G3923 De 2003
   [Fic]—dc21

                      2002006865

ISBN   0-7613-1727-9 (trade edition)
10 9 8 7 6 5 4 3 2 1

ISBN   0-7613-2813-0 (library binding)
10 9 8 7 6 5 4 3 2 1

Book design by BTDNYC
Printed in the United States of America
First edition

Always and always and always
For
Jim Giles and Josh Jakubik
My heroes

Acknowledgments

Many thanks yet again to the editor goddess, Deborah Brodie, to Simon Boughton and all the wonderful people at Roaring Brook Press. You've given me a home. Thank you, Scott Treimel, for taking care of business so I don't have to. Thanks to Deb Vanasse, Betty Monthei, Cynthia Leitich Smith, and Carolyn Crimi for reading early versions of this book. Rhonda Sexton for letting me use her first name. Pam Whitlock for just being Pam Whitlock. You've kept me going, my friend. Dawn Jakubik for being there for my son and being Hunter's mom. And to Hunter Jakubik for being. And one more time, Jimmy Buffett for writing "Changing Channels." The song got me off my fanny.

Chapter One

T hings had been getting a little better until I got a letter from my dead sister.

That more or less ruined my day.

It was Friday, the sun was out, but it wasn't yet in its usual Texas mean mood.

Mom had had a good night. Only one sleeping pill, so she was semigroggy rather than stumbling, mumbling, and weeping. No word from Dad for a while. Yes, it was a pretty good day.

I'd buzzed home during lunch break. Mr. Preston, the principal, knew the home-front situation and approved my request for an off-period combined with lunch. The drill was: I came home, checked Mom and the mail, ate my lunch, left some for Mom, made any calls that had to be made, forged a note from Mom saying I'd been there, then scooted back to school in time to hear other kids' crybaby bullshit about curfews.

Poor dears.

Today's mail consisted of a clutch of white envelopes with cellophane windows and a couple of catalogs. As I pulled the pile out in one bunch, a small yellow envelope slipped out and fluttered to the ground. Gracefully, just like my sister.

I froze, staring at the pale yellow rectangle. There's no way, I thought. She's dead. Dead girls don't write letters. Dead girls definitely don't write letters on yellow stationery. Dead girls might appear in dreams, they might make weird phantom ESP phone calls, but they do *not* write letters.

But Jazz had a flair for making a dramatic entrance. And she liked to write letters. And she used yellow stationery, the color of jasmine, the flower that was her namesake.

I bent and took the edge of the envelope in two fingers. As I turned it over, the return address leaped out at me. "Jasmine." Nothing else.

It was just like her. The whole world is supposed to know where Jazz Reynolds is.

I blinked into the sun, and recovered. Everyone does know where Jazz is. Dead, but not buried. This letter must have survived the fire, then lost its way, arriving months after the fact. I exhaled, not realizing I had been holding my breath, and my heart beat again. Everything was fine.

Sliding the small rectangle into my pocket, I hurried to the house. Mom didn't need to see the letter. Who knew how much Prozac it would take to counteract it. I paused on the steps. I ought to pitch it. Who could it help? Letters from dead girls never carry good news.

But it could be the last thing we'd ever have of Jazz. That thought scraped my conscience, so I sighed and continued through the kitchen door.

"Mom?"

"Here." Her voice wavered, as if she talked underwater. I knew she'd been crying. Again. Still.

I followed the sound into the living room. Mom sat on the sofa in her beige chenille bathrobe, her home-hacked hair unwashed. She wore pink-and-white rabbit slippers. A gift from Jazz. She leaned on her hand, tears running down her cheeks onto her fingers and down her wrists,

3

soaking into the cuffs of the ratty robe. On her lap was a scrapbook. Jazz's scrapbook.

I squatted next to the brown velveteen camel-backed couch. It used to be brocade, but I had thrown up on it so many times when I was a baby that it had to be re-covered. So this incarnation was my age, fourteen, and showing a lot of wear.

The couches reflected the differences between Jazz and me. I'd seen the pictures of Jazz perched sedately on emerald green brocade. Now it was utilitarian, blending into the dark wood floor.

I touched Mom's wrist to let her know I was close.

"Mom, you promised you wouldn't look at the scrapbook today. We agreed that you'd only look at it for an hour a week, remember?"

I had to whisper. A loud voice spooked Mom, and like a horse hearing a rattlesnake, it would set her galloping.

"Haven't had my hour this week." Mom's voice was weak and reedy.

"No, Mom. You looked at it yesterday and the day before. You promised you wouldn't look at it today."

I knelt and eased the book from Mom's lap. "Let me put it away. You promised to wash your hair and get dressed today. You said you'd eat lunch with me in the kitchen."

"Oh." Nothing else. One flat syllable.

The day sped downhill fast.

"Mom, have you had your pill this morning? I left it on your nightstand."

"Yes. Took it. Always take it."

I stood and carried the book with me as I hauled my butt upstairs. I turned into my room, slid the scrapbook under my bed, and trekked down the hall into Mom's room. The pill and the water glass lay untouched on her night table.

"Great, she's too depressed to take antidepressants."

I talked out loud a lot. Otherwise, there was nobody sane to talk to. I scooped up the pill and the water and scurried downstairs. Mom hadn't moved. Head still on hand, tears still flowing.

"Here, you must have forgotten." I handed Mom the pill.

"Just. Put it. Table. I'll. In a minute."

"Do me a favor and take it now, all right?" I reminded myself not to let my impatience show. It slowed things down. I put the pill into Mom's limp hand. I raised her hand to her mouth, and tapped the hand that cradled her head with the water glass. "Here, drink up."

"Miss her so much." Mom lifted her head and took the glass. Placing the pill on her tongue, she took a sip of water and swallowed. "I wish I could wake up just one morning and it never would have happened. I miss her so much."

"I know you miss her. Everybody does."

Yes, indeedy. Everybody misses Jazz.

Everybody but me.

Chapter Two

While I have problems feeling like part of my family, I do feel a kinship with our house. It is an old farmhouse, a no-frills kind of place. Brick floors, butcher-block countertops, and a baker's rack with Dad's cookbooks from his gourmet phase. Glass-door cabinets that I actually enjoy keeping spotless. Washing dishes and cleaning soothes me. Or maybe it's just that I see some kind of result from that labor.

I stood at the sink, scooping the insides out of tomatoes, then filling them with tuna salad. I placed crackers on the plate, popped ice cubes into the glasses, and poured tea. Smack in the center of the kitchen, Mom drooped, gazing at her plate.

"Jazz always put a sprig of mint in the tea." Her voice held a mixture of nostalgia and criticism.

My jaw muscles clenched. I opened my mouth and moved my lower jaw from side to side. It's a relaxation technique the dentist taught me for TMJ. TMJ is a warfare of muscles caused by stress. It gives me headaches that wrap me in a vise of pain.

"Yeah, Mom. I remember."

"Jazz had a touch, you know. Everything she did was, I don't know. . . special."

"Yeah, special. Try to eat, Mom."

"There wasn't anything Jazz couldn't do."

Nope, I thought. Not even die.

I watched Mom maul her lunch for a minute, then trotted back upstairs. I eased the yellow envelope out of my pocket and squinted at the writing. No mistake. Jazz's handwriting. Loose, flowing, and large, it whipped across the surface like a horse's mane in the wind.

Something kept me from opening the letter. I had a bad feeling. I decided I would honor the family's creed of non-confrontation.

"Well," I said to my bedroom walls, "it's waited this

long. It can wait a little longer." I tucked the envelope into my thesaurus and clattered down the stairs.

"Gonna be late. Finish your lunch, Mom, and promise you'll get dressed." I called out the words as I pushed through the screen door. I didn't wait for an answer.

The rest of the day I skated. I willed myself into a state of selective amnesia about the letter, Mom, and Jazz.

I attended afternoon classes cocooned in isolation. In small towns like Angleton, tragedy was a certain and direct way to celebrity. *Notoriety* might be a better word. People treated me as if I were contagious, carrying the catastrophe virus, but then again, they were shot full of *smug* that they had dodged the bullet and I was the bull's-eye.

At school, as everywhere, I was Jazz Reynolds's little sister. Never Sunny Reynolds. I had a few school friends before Jazz died, but none were close. I didn't make friends easily. Well, I didn't make friends at all. After living with a master of manipulation and deceit, I found it hard to believe anyone could be worthy of my trust.

Books were my best friends. They are there when you need them, and when you shut them, they stay closed.

As for teachers, before Jazz died—BJD—I was a source of disappointment to them. Jazz was silk, and I was cheesy polyester, the kind that makes you sweat and itch.

AJD—after Jazz died—I was treated with kid gloves. The

teachers tiptoed around me, avoiding any mention of the tragedy, wondering what they would do if, in one of their classes, I suddenly went crazy as a shithouse rat.

I overheard a conversation once between two of my teachers as they sauntered down the hall, carrying their stained coffee cups. Printed on one of the cups was THE THREE BEST THINGS ABOUT TEACHING: JUNE, JULY, AND AUGUST.

"That talented Reynolds girl. Killed so tragically."

"Heard her remains couldn't be identified. Nothing but ashes. "

"And the poor mother, having that breakdown."

"And the father. The only time he's not drinking is when he's passed out in jail."

"He was such a good journalist. The paper hasn't been the same without his column."

"The sister isn't nearly as bright as the one who died, is she?"

"No, and so plain, too."

They parted then, never seeing me behind them, and shuffled off to the next class to pass out papers and words of wisdom.

I could never decide which I hated most, school or home.

Mom was asleep when I got home. Tucking a crocheted throw around her, I flipped the TV on and watched the news. I love the reporter with totally fake white hair. When something is fake, I want it to look that way. He does stories about slick restaurants with rats and roaches and lots of gross stuff in their kitchens.

Later, I heated vegetarian vegetable soup in the microwave and ate it while I read my English assignment, a poem by Edgar Allan Poe, "Annabel Lee." Story of a man who ruined his life because he couldn't get over a dead girl.

Bet she didn't write letters.

I slapped the book shut. I washed my bowl and spoon and returned to the television. I channel surfed to find a horror movie or an exposé program, but had to settle for sitcoms with cute little kids doing cute little things in loving families. My eyes glazed over, and I called it a night.

Rather than wake Mom, I fetched a pillow from upstairs, slid it under her head, and retucked the light cover.

"I've tucked in the baby, the kitchen is clean, and I've done my homework." Huffing a big sigh, I headed upstairs. I'd put it off as long as I decently could. I had to read Jazz's last words.

I sat on my bed and pulled the letter from the thesaurus. Tapping it against my palm, I turned it over and over in my hands. I dropped the letter onto the bed.

I'd bathe first. The old-fashioned tub, the kind with lion's-claw feet clutching a big ball, was deep, and the hot water eased the crawling dread and flushed my skin when I slid in. I worked my jaw and rolled my head, stretching out the bunched muscles in my shoulders. I curled and uncurled my toes as I dumped shampoo on my hair. Washing my hair was an excuse to massage my scalp; the hot water and the kneading fingers told the scalp to relax, to lie gently across my forehead and temples.

I soaked until the water cooled, then toweled briskly and wrapped my hair turban-style. Pulling a long T-shirt from a cabinet in the bathroom, I slid it over the bulky headdress, removed the towel, and used it to buff the excess moisture from my hair. I dragged a wide-toothed comb through my straight, chin-length bob, and called it finished.

I always did these things in that order. I was a creature of lists, routines, and habit. Change and chaos. They were twins of different mothers.

I clicked on the bedside lamp, doused the overhead light, pulled back the soft cotton sheets, slid under, rearranged the pillows, and stared at the yellow envelope. I drummed my fingers against the paper, then snatched it up and ripped the envelope along the top edge. Tugging the letter from the envelope, I opened the folded pages. The first thing I saw was the date. Scrawled in Jazz's unmistakable writing was *May 20.*

It couldn't be. Jazz died in February. How could she write a letter in May, only four days ago?

Dear Mom, Dad, and Sunny,

I'm sure you are shocked to receive this letter. Like Mark Twain, I'm glad to say that the reports of my death have been greatly exaggerated. I know, I shouldn't be so glib about this, but, frankly, I don't know how to break the news to my family that I'm not dead after all.

I decided to write rather than call, hoping that the shock wouldn't be as bad this way.

This is what happened. My roommate and I hadn't been getting along. Lots of sniping and arguing. A friend told me that she could get me work with a repertory company in Vermont. The star's understudy was having a nose job and there was some reshuffling. It would be about ten weeks' work. I thought it would be a great idea. It would help if Rhonda (my roommate) and I had some time apart, and I needed the money. I needed some stage credits on my resume too.

So, off I went.

The fire didn't make the news, or I just didn't see it. I didn't know that I had been reported dead until I got back to New York. Imagine my surprise when I came back to find the apartment building had burned down. I got a room at the Y, and it was a couple of days before I managed to track down some friends. They were more than a little stunned to see me. In fact, it was seeing how shocked they were that persuaded me to write instead of call.

My friends told me the police were still trying to make positive identification, but it was slow because so many people died. Grim, isn't it? Anyway, it was assumed that I was a victim because my name was on the lease and no one had heard from me. I guess my habit of taking off without telling a soul has brought you all a lot of grief.

I went to the police and reported myself as living, and told them that I would inform you of my condition myself. Please consider yourself informed. I am alive and well.

I know that all this must have been terrible for you. I am coming to town so you can see for yourself that I am fine. I haven't much money, so I'll be on the bus. I'll be there Sunday at about noon. Don't come to the station. I want to see you all first at home. Please, it's important to me. Call Dad and ask him to be there too, okay?

See you soon, with bells on my toes.

Jazz

I folded the note and tried to stuff it back into the envelope. My hands shook, and I couldn't get the darned thing in. Once you let the genie out of the bottle . . .

Mom would be happy. With Jazz back, she might be able to pull her life together. Dad might dry out. Everybody's life would be like a sitcom. So why didn't I feel relieved?

I knew I should go down, wake Mom, and tell her. It was only nine o'clock. I should call Dad. I should be happy. I should love Jazz. Jazz, the great and powerful. But like Oz, there was a liar and a fraud hiding behind the curtain.

I reached under the bed and pulled out the scrapbook. Jasmine Reynolds. Her life and times. I flipped through the pages of the scrapbook, then slapped it shut, closing Jazz out. I shoved the book off the bed and snuggled down into the pillows and sheets.

Worm. That's what Jazz called me when nobody else was in earshot. Short for *worm food*. All I was good for, she said.

I remembered one night when I was ten and Jazz was fourteen. She was on her way to the movies with friends and had been told to take me along. She told me she was going to steal money from Dad's wallet to buy treats for her friends.

I was not quite horrified. Even at ten, I figured the money might as well go to Jazz's chocolate binge instead of one of Dad's binges. I knew Dad was a lush. I was one of those kids who heard and saw it all. One of the perks of being invisible. When Jazz was on the planet, it was like having a flash go off in your eyes. Nobody noticed me while they were Jazz-blind.

"But he'll know the money is gone, and he'll never be drunk enough to think Mom took it."

"I know how to handle it," she said.

"What are you going to do, blame me?" Already the burgeoning cynic.

"No, I'll tell him I did it."

She wasn't lying. When she was ready to leave, Dad went to the table by the front door where he always stowed his wallet and keys.

"Let me give you some money, Jazz." He flipped the wallet open, snagged a couple of bills, and handed them to her.

"That's odd." He pulled out all the bills and counted them.

His face darkened. "Did one of you take twenty dollars out of my wallet?"

I, like a primed pump, got a guilty look.

Jazz turned to me. "Sunny?" she asked quietly. Then she turned quickly to Dad.

"I did, Dad. I took the money," she said.

My eyes popped open in amazement. And that affected Dad just as Jazz planned.

"You did?" Dad said, staring straight at me but speaking to Jazz. "Why?"

"I wanted money for the movie," Jazz said.

I could see now, way too late, of course, how this was going.

"Dad, she—"

Jazz interrupted. "Sunny, hush. I'll . . ." She paused. "Be quiet. I want to do this."

She turned back to Dad. "I wanted to buy candy and stuff for the others."

My face was hot, and I was certain it was red.

"Sunny, what do you know about this?" Dad asked.

"She took it. Just like she said. But she's making it look like it was me," I whined. I knew I'd already lost.

"Right, she took the money and put the blame on you by admitting that she took it. Sounds a little Machiavellian to me. Do you know who Machiavelli is?"

I didn't, but I was fairly certain he was related to Jazz.

"But, Dad, I did. I took the money," Jazz said.

"Stop covering for her, Jazz. She not only took it, she's blaming you. Why should you try to help her?"

"She's my sister," Jazz said.

Dad got so mad when I wouldn't cough up the twenty that he ordered me to my room. I spit and hissed, making it worse for myself, then trudged upstairs. But not before Jazz flashed her smug smile at me as she flounced out the door, without my troublesome presence, but with Dad's twenty, as well as his goodwill.

I dragged myself back to the present and looked at the letter one more time.

I'll tell them all tomorrow. I wanted one more night without Jazz.

Chapter Three

"Wake up. I've got something to tell you." I shook Mom's shoulder.

Mom muttered something, then draped one arm over her eyes.

I gripped her chin. "Come on, wake up."

A deep sigh was her only response.

"How many sleeping pills did you take?" I pushed my hair off my face with my forearm.

Another sigh.

"Fine, I'll call Dad. He'll get the news first, and won't that rattle your knees."

I snatched the phone from its place on a round side table, put my back to the wall, and slid down until I sat on the floor. Clamping the receiver between ear and shoulder, I plunked the base in my lap and jabbed the buttons. I heard it ring.

"C'mon, Dad. Answer. I know you've got a hangover, but I'm gonna let this puppy ring until your head explodes, so answer."

On the twelfth ring, I heard the receiver lift, then a loud thump rattled my eardrum. Dad had knocked the phone onto the floor.

Oh, yeah, last night must have been a *real* Big Time. Galloping my fingers against the dark oak-planked floor, I waited as the phone was fumbled, lost, clanked, and clattered. I really drew wild cards from the gene pool. A drunk, a pill head, and Lazarus. What a pretty family.

"Yeah, what?" Dad's voice was shaky and cross.

"Dad?"

"Yeah, sort of. What time is it?"

"Dad, I need to talk to you, right now."

"Sunny, give your old man a break. I can't read the numbers on the clock."

"Can you read the letters on the bottle? I'll bet they say 'Jack Daniel's.'" I wasn't angry, just tired. This was too much trouble.

"Sunn, if you want to complain about your drunken

lout of a father, go to an Al-Anon meeting." He was just
as tired.

"I know it's early, but this is important. Can you come
over here?"

I heard a long, deep sigh and a soft sound that I recognized as Dad scrubbing his hand over beard stubble.
"Nothing's so important that it can't wait until the crack of
noon. Just tell me. I can't come over there and listen to
your mother weep and wail and gnash her teeth at me."

I waited a beat to get his attention.

"Dad, I got a letter from Jazz."

The phone clattered to the floor again. I replaced the
receiver in the cradle.

Bingo, world's first hangover cure.

I hustled Mom into a shower, bundled her into a clean
terrycloth robe, steered her down the stairs, propped her
in a chair, and pushed a mug of coffee under her nose.

"Drink up. Dad will be here in a minute."

"Don't want . . . talk to him," Mom whined.

My jaw muscles knotted. "Fine, don't talk to him.
Listen to me. I'll be doing the talking."

I felt a twinge of guilt. I was being pretty rough with her,
but soon they'd forget I had been impatient with them.
After this news, they'd forget me altogether.

Mom gripped the mug with both hands. "Don't. Be hateful. Had a bad night." Her voice was weak and whispery. "I think I'm having a reaction to my medication or something." It was a rehearsed statement I had heard all too often. On her bad days, it was one of the only complete sentences in Mom's repertoire.

A feeble knock at the back screen door made us look up.

"That's Dad. Keep drinking your coffee. I need you to understand what I'm going to tell you." I went to the door and pulled it wide.

"It wasn't locked," I told Dad.

"And it's not my house now," he answered. He looked like the old cliché, miles of bad road, unshaven, haggard, his eyes red and watering. "Why'd you hang up? What did you mean you got—"

I broke in. "I'll tell you both. Sit down, have some coffee."

"Hate the stuff. It sobers me up and then I have to start drinking again." He dragged out a chair, wincing at the squeak of the heavy wooden Shaker chair against the kitchen's brick floor. "Morning, Lily. Glad to see someone looks as bad as I do."

Mom put one hand to her brow, as if shielding her eyes from light. She said nothing.

Reaching up, I pulled the note from its hiding place on

the top of the refrigerator. Toulouse, our cat, swatted at my fingers. He had a preference for high places. I took the envelope with the folded pages still flapping partially out and laid it on the pine tabletop.

"This came in the mail yesterday."

Mom continued shielding her eyes, but Dad took the envelope. "It's from Jazz." He said it like a prayer.

Mom made a small sound, deep in her throat.

Caressing the envelope with his fingertips, Dad's eyes welled with tears. "It's from Jazz," he said again.

I massaged my jaw, then crossed my arms over my chest and leaned back against the sink.

Mom's hand fluttered away from her face. "Jazz?" she muttered.

"Mom and Dad, Jazz is alive." I waited. Silence. I heard Toulouse purr. What kind of cat purrs to itself?

"You're . . . ummm . . . stunned. Me, too." Still no response. I was talking to statues.

"She says in the letter that she was away all this time working in a repertory company. She didn't know about the fire or that she had been reported dead."

Still nothing. Dad turned the envelope over. Mom stared, eyes wide, as if afraid of it.

"Mom, Dad. Do you hear me? Jazz is alive. She'll be here tomorrow."

Tears raced each other down Mom's cheeks. She moved

her fingers toward the envelope but stopped short of touching it. "Jazz?"

Dad looked as if he'd been hit with something large and lethal. He sat forward, his elbows on the table, the yellow envelope now on the table between them.

"Is this true?" Hope and joy were sneaking their way into his tone. "Sunny, is Jazz really. . . ?"

He can't let himself believe it, I thought. It's that big for him. He's like someone who has been in an earthquake and when everything quits shaking doesn't know how to stand.

"Dad, you know as much as I do. The letter was in the box yesterday." I paused. "I ignored it. I figured it was an old letter that just got here, and I didn't want to read it right away." A small lie was in order right about here, I thought. "I didn't read it until this morning."

Dad's nod was vague, like a man still finding his balance. He pulled the pages loose from the envelope and spread them out.

"It's her handwriting."

"Yeah, and the return address is just 'Jasmine.' She always did that, and the yellow stationery. Everything fits."

Dad took a deep breath. It inflated him like a balloon man, pulled him upright, made him firm instead of hollow. "Then you think she might really be . . . alive."

Once Dad said it, I knew it was true. "Yeah, Dad. I think she's alive."

I expected my parents to fall into each other's arms, booing and hooing with relief. I was stunned by the continued silence.

"Jasmine, my Jazz is coming home?"

I saw that Mom's tears had saturated the rolled collar on her thick robe. "Yeah, Mom, that's what Dad and I think." I closed my eyes and rubbed the lids with my fingertips.

"She's coming home?" Mom's words, lost and hopeful, echoed along the brick floor. *Home, home, home.*

Dad scraped back his chair and crossed the kitchen. He pulled out a mug and filled it with coffee.

"Yes, she's coming home, Lily. Get over the lost little girl routine. You're going to be a mother again. Maybe you should dress the part."

I felt like I had been sucker punched.

I headed for the door. "I'll let you guys read the letter and make your plans." My tone was cold and hard. Like their hearts.

"Sunn, I don't get you," Dad said. "What's with the attitude? It's as if you don't want Jazz to come home."

Dad's tone wasn't lost or wavering now. He was intense, probing. The journalist had risen from the grave.

Lots of resurrections today.

"I'm just like you and Mom." I scrounged for more words. I needed to get out of this room. Out of this house. "It's hard to take it all in. I need to see her before I can let myself trust it."

Rubbing the hot mug across his forehead, probably trying to ease a headache, Dad seemed mollified. "Yeah, I guess so. And you've had a chance to get over the initial shock."

"Sure." I pushed through the heavy swinging door, sprinted though the dining and living rooms, and banged my way outside. In the gardening shed, I snatched a heavy shovel and, without slowing, sped to the mailbox. Hefting the shovel in a two-handed batter's grip, I swung it once, then again and yet again. I didn't stop swinging until the mailbox was crushed and broken on the ground.

Chapter Four

No one noticed the untimely demise of the mailbox. No one noticed that I spent the rest of the day in my room. No one noticed diddly. Things were right back to normal.

I came down that evening to find a bucket of Kentucky Fried Chicken on the kitchen table. A wing and a leg were left abandoned in the bottom of the bucket. Mom, still in her robe, pulled groceries from plastic bags and arranged them on the counter.

"I can start the roast at about ten. I'll mash the potatoes right before dinner and make the gravy then, too. Jazz likes the green beans steamed, so those will have to wait. I'll make brownies tonight."

She glanced over her shoulder at me. "I got fudge ripple ice cream to put on the brownies." Opening the refrigerator, she placed the roast on a shelf, thumped the beans next to it, then pulled lettuce, tomato, and red onion from the sack. "She likes brownies warm, but I can microwave them for a few seconds and they'll be fine. Don't you think?"

Mom spoke in complete sentences, but she spoke to the roast, the air, or the cat, so I didn't bother to answer. She was close to manic, and I knew a crash lurked. I snapped a paper towel off the roll and sat down. "Where'd the groceries come from?" I asked.

Mom continued stocking the refrigerator.

"Did Dad go shopping for you?"

"I didn't ask him. It was for Jasmine. We both wanted to have all her favorite foods."

Mom shut the refrigerator and clattered in the cabinets for the brownie pan.

"He called the bus station. The only bus Jazz could be on is the twelve-fifteen."

"So, you two decided to go whole hog."

"I don't know why you are always so sullen, Sunny. Why can't you be more like your sister?"

"Just lucky, I guess." I wadded the uneaten chicken into the paper towel and pitched it at the garbage can. "I'm going to my room. I have a book I want to finish."

The next day, I put on overalls, a clean white T-shirt, and sneakers, and came downstairs at eleven-thirty. Mom and Dad paced around the living room. The place was as clean as I'd ever seen it. The floor gleamed with a fresh coat of lemon oil, and the worn couch was brushed to respectability. The pillows, throws, and newspaper had vanished, and the television in the corner was turned off. The wing-backed chair facing the room seemed bigger, lighter, even though the curtains were drawn tight. The air was redolent with the smells of garlic, onion, roast, and fresh bread.

The oval of etched glass in the front door sparkled, the end tables were dusted, and the pictures on the walls were straight. Pictures of Jazz at three in a tutu, at seven in her Brownie uniform, at sixteen in her cheerleader's uniform, at eighteen in a satin gown being crowned Homecoming Queen. There were a couple of me, too. Most taken when I was a baby. One was taken when I was four and Jazz was eight. She stood, ready for church in a kicky plaid kilt and pristine white blouse. Smiling. I was next to her, my face twisted in a knot of fury. I wore a flowered dress. I remembered it. A dress was bad enough, but a sissy-girly dress with pink flowers? No way. Why didn't I have a cool kilt with an even cooler oversized gold safety pin holding it primly closed? Mom and Dad called it the Angel and the Devil portrait.

"Why aren't you dressed?" Dad demanded.

"Excuse me, am I naked again?" I crossed the dining room and went into the kitchen. I snagged a can of Coke as I surveyed the room. The brownies were on the counter, the potatoes simmered gently on the burner, and the serving dishes were stacked and ready. I shook my head. Mom had pulled out Granny Wilson's china.

Popping the tab of my Coke, I returned to the living room and slouched into the wing-backed chair.

"Sunny, you know I hate it when you toss off a smart remark and then leave the room. It's the act of a coward."

"Yeah, right, Dad. And crawling into a bottle of whiskey is the act of a hero. Thanks for the lesson."

"Sunny, don't speak to your father like that." Mom's tone was distracted and lacked spirit. An autopilot kind of behavior-modification attempt. Mom stood at the window, watching the driveway through a narrow gap in the curtain. She twisted her fingers.

"I'm going to ignore that," Dad said. "I don't want to

spoil the day with an argument. Answer me. Why aren't you dressed?"

"I *am* dressed."

"You look like you're going to plow the north forty."

"I thought we were expecting Jazz, not royalty. Why does it matter how I'm dressed?"

Dad rubbed his hands against his knees. "Why do you always have to be so difficult? You've always been this way. You just—"

I cut him off. "I got all the bad DNA, what can I say?" I swigged my Coke. "Sit down, Mom. The bus isn't even here yet."

"Yes, it is. Dan called the station. The bus was early." She put her hands to her mouth. "Dan, there's a cab. She's here."

I heard tires crunch on the crushed-shell drive, and my stomach lurched.

Dad bolted to his feet and strode to the front door. He opened it and looked toward Mom. She backed away from the window, distancing herself from the opened door. Shrugging, Dad pushed past the screen door onto the porch.

I stayed in my chair but placed the Coke on the floor.

I heard a squeal. "Dad, oh, I'm so glad you're here." There was no answer from Dad. Light steps pattered up the wooden stairs. The door opened, a large carpetbag suitcase thumped in, followed by a tall, slim shape that entered with a swirling pirouette. *"Ta da!* I'm home!" The light silhouetted the shape and cast the face in shadow.

She wore clunky black boots, a long skirt, and a white silk blouse. Her dark hair framed her shadowed face and brushed her shoulders.

"Mom, come give me hug. I'm home!" She stepped forward out of the shadow.

It wasn't Jazz.

Chapter Five

I rose from the chair, then stuck like a stopped watch. I stared as this person, who was not Jazz, swept across the living room to my astonished mother. She was taller than Jazz. Her hair was dark and straight like Jazz's, but Jazz had bangs and this girl didn't. From a distance she looked like Jazz. But the face was wrong. She was prettier than Jazz, her skin a little softer, her lashes longer and darker. Jazz was pretty; this girl was stunning. Her face held a hint of vulnerability that my sister's never had.

Reaching out, Not-Jazz took Mom's hands in her own, pressing them to her cheeks.

"Mom? You look like you're seeing a ghost, but I promise, I'm not a ghost at all. See, flesh and bone." The Not-Jazz girl let Mom's hands drop and put her own hands to Mom's cheeks. "Look at me, Mom. It's me, your Jasmine."

Mom stood, shell-shocked and teary-eyed. "Jazz?" Her eyes drifted around the room, looking for an anchor. I could only return her pleading look with one of bafflement. Dad came in from the porch. His shoulders sagged, and he walked as if the ground had shifted under his feet.

"Oh, Mom, it's so good to be home." Not-Jazz pulled Mom into her arms and hugged her. Mom was stiff and wooden for a moment, then her arms rose tentatively. She broke into great hiccuping sobs, encircled Not-Jazz's shoulders, and hugged the girl fiercely.

"Oh, Jazz, Jazz, you're home. You're home." They sobbed in each other's arms.

What was happening here?

Not-Jazz pulled back and wiped Mom's tears with the balls of her thumbs. "Look at us. Two weeping Nellies. That's what Grandpa Wilson would call us."

My world took another tilt. How did this girl know about Grandpa Wilson? How did she know that expression, a favorite of Grandpa's?

Not-Jazz turned and saw me. "Sunn, give your big sister a hug." She hurried across and grabbed me, twirling me around. Ever smooth, I stumbled into the can of Coke, knocking it over.

"Oh, my gosh, that's my fault," Not-Jazz said. She giggled. Her laugh sounded like rain on a tin roof, its cadence soothing and quick. "Well, Mom, I guess that 'grace and elegance' thing isn't holding true these days."

Dad's sharp intake of breath was audible across the room. We stared at each other, astonishment competing with confusion. Jasmine, specifically yellow jasmine, was the symbol of grace and elegance. Mom had a favorite book, *The Language of Flowers*, and had named us from its pages.

Who was this girl? How did she know these things?

Not-Jazz patted my head. "Don't sweat, Cheekums. I'll clean it up." She darted to the kitchen without so much as a glance for directions. "Cheekums" was a baby nickname I hated. My grandmother slapped it on me because I had chubby, round cheeks as a child.

Who was this girl?

Mom sank down on the sofa. "She's home. Jasmine is back home. The Lord has been good to us."

And I thought, when I got Jazz's letter, that things couldn't get worse.

Not-Jazz pranced back into the living room with a wad

of paper towels. She looked as if she were carrying a bouquet of chrysanthemums. Stooping, she swiped and blotted at the puddle.

"I know, you guys are in shock to see me clean anything." She popped up, grinning. "Folks, I'm not the Jazz you remember."

That's proof. This girl told the truth, something the real Jazz never got the hang of.

Not-Jazz flashed back into the kitchen and returned without the towels. "Yeah, living on your own changes things. If I left something undone, no little elves or an overworked mother took care of it for me."

We stood around "with our faces hanging out," as Grandpa Wilson used to say. I waited for someone, anyone, to say, "And who the hell are you?"

"Sunn, you look fabulous. Your outfit is the biggest thing in New York. All you'd have to do is switch the sneakers for patent-leather Mary Janes and you could greet royalty."

I couldn't resist a "so there" glance at Dad. I didn't know who this Not-Jazz was, but I found myself preferring her to the real one.

"Look, I don't know what's going on here, but—" Dad was caught in mid-sentence by Mom's voice. A new Mom, one who sounded competent and sure.

"Dan, don't start on Jazz. I'm sure she's worn-out."

Mom pushed her way to the slender girl and stroked her hair. "A bus ride from New York is long and exhausting. I'll bet Jasmine would like a nap before dinner."

"Oh, Mom, you always look out for your little girl." Not-Jazz kissed Mom's cheek. "I would like to take a shower and change. I feel travel grungy, you know?" She stepped past Dad and shouldered her bag. "I won't be too long. I saw and smelled all my favorites in the kitchen, and I'm famished." Her smile could charm cobras. "You know me, eat like a truck driver." She took the stairs two at a time. "Back in a flash."

We watched as this stranger turned without hesitation into Jazz's room.

"Isn't she beautiful? I knew the Lord couldn't be cruel enough to take my child without even a chance to say good-bye." Mom stood and clasped her hands against her chest, her eyes gazing up the stairs.

She whirled, hugging herself, eyes glowing through unshed tears.

"My Jasmine is back. I'll never complain about anything ever again."

Dad stepped close to Mom, touching her shoulder as if stroking the feathers of a delicate-boned bird.

"Lily, honey, don't you see—"

Mom cut him short, slapping his hand away, her face and voice fierce. "I see our girl, home where she belongs. I won't hear any of your drunken blathering. If you can't accept the work of the Lord, then get out of this house." She marched to the kitchen, flinging words over her shoulder. "I need to set the table and warm the food. And those green beans need steaming."

We stared at each other. I broke eye contact first and slumped back into the wing-backed chair. Shambling to the couch, Dad sank into the cushions with a sigh. He sat, elbows on knees, kneading his eyes with the heels of his palms. All the sounds in the house grew louder. I heard the whine of water rushing through the pipes as the stranger who knew us and knew our house showered upstairs. I heard my mother singing bits of show tunes and rattling silverware. I heard my father's deep, ragged breath and my own heart pounding.

"You know it's not her, don't you?" Dad didn't stop rubbing his eyes. His head was still down.

"Yeah. It's not Jazz."

"Thanks, I was wondering if the booze had finally sent me out where the buses don't run."

"Dad, how does she know all this stuff?" I leaned forward, intense. "She knows us, she knows this house, she knows all kinds of stuff about us. It's spooky."

"Yeah. I saw her when she got out of the cab, and my heart just stopped. It wasn't her. Made me wonder which one of us was crazy."

"She was glad to see me, *and* she was nice to me. That's proof she's not Jazz," I said.

Dad bolted to his feet. "Your sister is dead. Can't you give the smart-assed remarks a rest?"

I looked at my feet. Seeing Mom absorb this girl, seeing this stranger suck all the air out of the room, was just like having Jazz here.

When I looked up, Dad stood at the foot of the stairs. He was holding the newel post and staring at Jazz's closed door.

"I'm sorry, Dad, I—"

"Her hair has the same smell. You know, when she hugged me. It smells like that stuff she uses."

He didn't hear me. It's that way when Jazz is here.

Then it struck me. Dad had spoken and I had thought in present tense.

Chapter Six

Dad dragged himself reluctantly away from the newel post.

"Sunny, I know this girl isn't Jazz. But I think we have to play along for a few hours."

"Play along?"

"I know how crushed I was when I saw her get out of that cab and realized Jazz wasn't coming back after all. If we force your mother to realize it, too, she's going to go over the edge. You heard her. She's convinced that's Jazz."

I nodded. "You could be right."

Dad rubbed his face in his chin-scrubbing motion.

Clear evidence he was in ponder mode. "I want to talk to Lily's doctor, see how she thinks we should handle this."

He looked at me, some of his old intensity resurfacing. "What's your take? Do you think this girl is dangerous?"

I wasn't sure if Dad was thinking out loud or if he deemed my opinion worthwhile.

"We've seen her for about ten minutes. How can we know?"

Dad was still hip deep in thought. "True."

"What's in it for her to hurt us?"

"That's a good point. We're self-destructing on our own."

Wasn't much I could add to that.

"There are too many questions, and I want answers. Let's play it by ear. Watch her, listen to her. See where she slips up. She's bound to, she can't know everything."

"Dad, this isn't a newspaper story. This is our life."

"Not up to it?"

That knocked out any good feeling I had going for him. I glared and tapped my foot against the wooden floor. My sneakers made a slapping noise, a Morse code of anger. I ground my teeth until the muscles in my jaw throbbed.

"Oh, great," Dad said. He stormed across the room and flung himself onto the couch. "The old passive-aggressive thing." He grabbed one of the pillows and slammed it against the rolled arm of the couch.

I might be passive-aggressive, but Dad and Mom were just passive. Dad was a reporter. A nonparticipant. Mom couldn't deal with putting on her clothes. It didn't matter what I thought—this girl, this impostor, was going to stay.

"Sunny, stop that damned stamping. Just once can't you do what I ask without sulking?"

I slammed both feet down and stood. "You got it. I'll go help set the table and make nice to my brand-new sister. Absolutely sulk-free."

I stormed past my father, ready to commit mayhem on a few more mailboxes.

Not-Jazz bounced down the stairs, slipped across the room, and hugged Dad.

Dad pulled back, but then bent his chin to her head. It hurt me to see longing on his face as he smelled her hair.

Mom burst back in, bread in hand. "Sit, sit, everybody. You know I hate for good food to get cold." Neither Dad nor I moved to the table. Not-Jazz waltzed to the left side of the table, like metal shavings to a magnet, and slid into the chair. Jazz's chair.

Dad and I exchanged glances and took our customary

places. Mom started passing dishes, apologizing as she worked. "Now, I'm afraid these potatoes might be a little lumpy. I just couldn't seem to—"

Not-Jazz interrupted. "—make those lumps behave. And I hope the gravy isn't too salty, you know what a heavy hand I have with the salt, and I just know this roast is going to be as tough as an old boot. . . ." The girl stopped and grinned. "You never change." She reached across the table and touched Mom's hand. "Thank goodness."

Whoever this was, she knew Jazz.

The girl filled her plate and chirped like a tree full of spring birds. "Dad, you'll love this story." She launched into a comical story about a Chinese New Year parade she had seen in New York. I watched and listened. The girl's voice wasn't Jazz's. My sister's voice had a slight rasp that men thought sexy, but set my teeth on edge. Jazz seemed to bite off the ends of her words, sharpening them, while Not-Jazz's voice was like satin ribbon sliding off a spool.

But the rest was familiar. Jazz had always lowered her voice and leaned in to people, as if imparting a personal secret. She pulled people in to her, spun a web around them, and kept them close.

I watched as Not-Jazz cut her meat and ate. Jazz was left-handed but in Catholic school left-handedness was frowned upon. Jazz had learned to do anything that related to school, things the nuns might see, right-handed. She ate European style, cutting with her right hand and eating with her left, fork tines pointed down. The nuns didn't argue with this, considering it acceptable. The new Jazz must have found it acceptable also, because she handled her knife and fork like Jazz's clone.

I glanced at Dad. He wasn't watching Jazz's fork or knife; he was chuckling at her story. This girl knew how to work him.

"So after the dragons and the lion-headed thing, there were bands and floats. Then I heard bagpipes. And there they were, an entire posse of kilted bagpipers. That's not all. Right behind them was a garbage truck." She turned to take in the rest of us. "I'm not making this up. A bona fide garbage truck, festooned with streamers." She turned back to Dad and leaned in, whispering like a conspirator.

"Now, I ask you, Dad, just when did bagpipes and kilts make their appearance in China? And a garbage truck? What dynasty do you think the garbage truck represented?" She giggled and made Jazz's "duh?" face.

The news of Jazz's death hadn't produced an earthquake. It had been an eclipse.

And my parents were blinded by this new light.

Chapter Seven

"So, Dad, how are Nasty and Grouchy these days?"

I jerked back from Jazz's words, dropping my fork. It bounced off the plate, slinging splatters of gravy onto the cloth.

"Sunny!" Mom's voice was sharp.

"Sorry, Mom, I—"

"Don't fuss at Sunny, Mom. It's my fault." Jazz was grinning like a cream-fed cat.

"I can't believe you said that." Dad tossed his head back and laughed. His rich laugh built on itself like soft summer thunder, bounced off the walls and floors, and produced double echoes in Not-Jazz and me.

"You're in for it now," Dad said, wiping his eyes with his napkin.

I laughed with him, wondering why it felt so good. This girl had just dropped a Scud missile on the table.

"Jasmine, I hate to be ugly to you on a day like this, but you know how I feel about that. All of you have been forbidden to call your grandmother that . . . name."

"And we've used it out of your earshot." Not-Jazz's face pinked with amusement. "We can't help it if your parents are escapees from a bad Faulkner novel. 'Grouchy' fits Grandpa Wilson to a T. And if Granny isn't—"

"Nasty." Mom said the word, eyes still locked on her plate. She covered her eyes with her fingers and her shoulders shook.

The mood clouded. Then Mom lifted her face and uncovered her eyes. "Oh, I hope the good Lord forgives us all. Nothing could fit the woman better." She rolled her eyes up and tried to suppress her grin.

"Remember when Grouchy said Nasty was so mean that he had to feed her with a slingshot?" I was caught up in the moment. "And what about the dog?"

Jazz filled in. "He said she made a junkyard dog look like the Easter bunny."

Mom waved her hand. "You don't know the half of it. When I was a child, Papa told me she could give me a look that would stunt my growth." Laughter welled back up. "And I believed him."

"Well, who wouldn't?" Jazz added. She crossed her fingers as if warding off a vampire.

"We're all going straight to hell for this," Mom said, trying to compose herself.

"Oh, I hope not." Dad sighed. "Think of being stuck with Nasty in the hereafter."

"Dan!" Lily swatted him with her napkin. "For heaven's sakes, try to set a good example."

I couldn't believe it. Mom was flirting.

"Mom, anything mean we've said, Nasty's already said about us," Jazz said.

"Yeah," Dad added, "and she's been saying it longer."

"What I want to know is, why would anyone name a baby 'Nasturtium'? That would make me mean, too," I said.

Mom looked at us. Nobody said a word.

Mom pushed back from the table. Her voice trembled and her eyes clouded. "It seems like Momma has spoiled yet another meal. I can't eat when she's at the table— whether she's sitting here or it's her mean spirit around." She turned to move toward the living room, swayed, and grasped the back of her chair.

"Lily," Dad bumped out of his chair, hitting the table with a knee. The crystal danced with the silver. He reached

Mom and cradled her against his shoulder. "Steady now."

Turning into his shoulder, Mom sobbed, "I don't . . . I just . . . I. . . ." She sobbed more, and muttered the worn-thin sentence: "I think I'm having a reaction to my medication or something."

Dad eased Mom into her chair and backed away from her confusion and pain. "Sunny, take care of your mother." He rubbed his hands against his pant legs, as if cleaning them. "She needs some quiet and some rest. I'd just upset her, so I'll . . . I'll go now." He backed away, as if fending us off, until he reached the swinging door into the kitchen. He darted through it, and quicker than a whisker twitch, I heard the screen door bang behind him.

"And the rat leaves the sinking ship," I said. "As always." I strode over to Mom. "You didn't take your pills last night or this morning, did you?"

"I don't . . . I . . . I mean. . . Jazz is back now and. . . ." Mom waved her fingers listlessly in front of her face. "I can't . . . don't . . . remember."

"Let's go upstairs, Mom. It's been a big day. You need to sleep." I helped my mother up and began steering her to the stairs.

"Maybe just a little lie-down." Mom tried out a wan smile. It shook and faltered before it made it to her lips. "Jazz, honey, I'm so glad. . . you're. . . glad that. . . ."

Jazz stroked Mom's hair. "I know, Mom. I know."

I herded Mom up the stairs and into her room, where I watched her swallow the pills and tucked her under the bedcovers as if she were a frail, frightened child.

"Have a nice nap, Mom. I'll take care of things downstairs."

"Jazz will still be . . . she won't . . . ?"

I sighed and rubbed the back of my neck. "No, Mom, Jazz won't go away again," I said. "She'll still be here."

Chapter Eight

When I came into the dining room, Jazz was closing the top drawer of the buffet.

"What are you looking for?" I asked.

"This tablecloth needs to be washed." She pointed to the gravy stains. "I was looking for another one."

"Leave it bare. We don't stand much on formality these days."

Jazz nodded and began clearing the table.

"Thanks for helping," I said.

"Sure," Jazz said. "How is she?"

My short laugh was a snort. "Compared to what?

Compared to world famine and genocide? Pretty chipper.
Compared to society's definition of normal?"

"Same old Sunny," Jazz said.

I felt like she'd splashed ice water in my face.

"And what would you know about it?" I demanded.

Jazz's smile was slow and sad. "Nothing, I guess."

"Yeah, I guess not."

Jazz sighed and shrugged her shoulders. "I left you with
this mess. I can't know what kind of hell you've been
through." Jazz gathered the silverware onto one plate and
started toward the kitchen. "I deserve every bit of bitter-
ness you have stored up." She glided from the room.

I clutched at a few pieces of stemware. That was close. I
had to make her think I believed her. I couldn't fly off
again. Jazz was comfortable with my anger. This girl might
not be. The crazy part was—I wanted her to like me. I followed her into the kitchen.

I put the crystal carefully on the counter. "Jazz, I didn't
mean—"

"Don't you dare apologize." Her smooth voice was calm
and soft. I felt myself moving closer to hear it. To be near it.

"We both know how selfish I am. I run away from an
ugly situation as fast as Mom and Dad do."

She ran water in the sink, reached unerringly into the
cabinet that housed sponges and detergent. Squeezing a

line of soap under the flowing water, she adjusted the faucets for more hot water and placed the silverware into the sink.

I watched, fascinated by the grace with which the girl moved. I noticed she used her right hand to turn faucets. Jazz used her left. At least I thought she did.

The girl closed the faucets and began washing the silverware. "Dad's a drunk and Mom's certifiable. I'm a coward." She turned to me, tears glazing her eyes. "I'm sorry, Sunn."

"What can you expect of yourself, Jazz? Look at the gene pool."

"It didn't seem to affect you. You're here."

"Where else could I go?"

"Right," Jazz said, and the tears slipped down her cheeks. She wiped her cheeks with her forearm and rinsed the forks. "I'm a selfish shit."

I shook my head. Left hand, right hand, what difference did it make? Jazz would never, never have said that.

We finished the dishes in silence, and Jazz told me she was tired and would like a nap while Mom rested. I agreed and went to my own room.

My room is a world made to my specifications. Like the kitchen, it shouts "stark." The twin bed is iron, painted white; the walls, white; the curtains, white and gauzy, letting the light in; the bedspread, white chenille. No fluff, no cutesy needlepoint pillows. No posters of rock stars or pictures of boyfriends. Bookshelves, chock-full, cover one wall. Over my bed hangs a framed print. A black-and-white photograph of an empty rowboat. With its oars shipped, it rests on still water, the bow pointed toward a storm building in the distance.

A night table holds my lamp and alarm clock. There's a desk made of a door resting on sawhorses—all painted white. A book about Leonardo da Vinci and a notebook where I practice his style of mirror-writing rest on it. A rocking chair stands next to the bed, and a door leads to a bathroom that connects my room to Jazz's. I hated it when Jazz lived here. She'd lock my side of the bathroom door from her side. Then I'd have to knock on her hallway door and beg to be let in. That was sport for Jazz.

I got the vacuum cleaner and pushed it across the floor. I needed to assess the situation. Get things in order.

In February, Ollie, our police chief, appeared at our door. He had a look on his face that said he'd rather dig his own grave than talk to us. He said NYPD had called and reported that Jazz's building had burned to the ground. While they couldn't make positive identification because of the number and condition of the bodies, Jazz had not

been seen in New York since the fire and she was presumed dead.

Dad and Mom refused to believe Jazz was dead. Dad called Ollie at work and at home constantly, but as the weeks wore on, denial got harder. When Jazz ran away to the city, they were shaken, and now their loose pieces fell apart.

Then a letter arrived. A letter from a dead girl. But the girl who arrived on the porch was not Jazz. Absolutely not Jazz.

Why was I playing this game? Why didn't I just hike in there and say, "You are not my dead sister." What would happen? Would she roll over and say, "Busted, I'm really Elvis!"

Why didn't I find out who she was and why she wanted to do this? I sighed. Because this girl was a Jazz I liked. A better, kinder Jazz.

Suddenly an idea zinged into my head. I turned off the vacuum. From the idea, a plan formed, a plan that could work. I'd caught sight of the tail, now I could follow it to the rat.

Chapter Nine

In the bathroom I cranked the faucets in the tub and started rooting in the cabinet. I pulled a jar of bath crystals from the back and spilled some into the water. I watched as the crystals foamed, swirled, and released a floral scent carried by the steam. I knocked on the adjoining door and called, "Jazz, it's me. Can I come in?"

"Sure."

I pushed the door open and stepped into Jazz's world. Her room resembled a gypsy's wagon. The walls were yellow, of course, but only slivers of color showed between the collage of posters, pictures, dried Homecoming mums, cheerleader pom-poms, prom tickets, and other Jazz-junk that was pinned, tacked, or taped to them. Scarves carelessly draped over lamps gave the room color and warmth. The dressing table was covered with framed photos, the Jazz hall of fame, and photos of her numerous boyfriends were stuck in the mirror frame. The bed was filled with multicolored pillows, and a mosquito net fell over the head of the bed, making it look like a queen's throne.

A megaphone, a CD player, stacks of CDs, stuffed animals that were presents from admiring high school sports heroes littered the room in haphazard abandon. Everything in the room was as whimsical as the black-and-white cat wall clock whose tail wagged and eyes shifted as the minutes passed. I hated that thing.

Jazz sat in front of the dressing table. She held a photograph and looked alternately at it and her reflection.

"I started a bath for you. I know you had a shower before, but there's nothing like a long soak in a hot tub," I said.

"Yeah, it's a great de-stressor." She turned to face me. "How do you do it? De-stress, I mean?"

"I read books like *Little Women* with perfect people in perfect families and wish I were there. I read books by people like Poe and King and think that we would be grist for their horror mill. I read travel books and—"

"I've got the picture." Jazz held up a photograph. "Look at this. I'm not the girl in this picture."

I suppressed a smirk. "How's that?"

"Other than I've lost weight and don't have these chubby cheeks, and I let my bangs grow out, there's more." She turned back to her reflection. "Coming back from the dead changes you. Only luck kept me from dying in the fire." She reached out and touched the mirror. "I was all surface, a pretty face." She laid down the photograph and spoke to my reflection. "How did you stand me?"

I looked at Jazz, dumbstruck. I tried to think of something to say, but nothing came. Then I remembered the rushing water in the bathroom.

"We're going to have to swim out of here if I don't turn off the water."

We bolted for the door. We tangled and went down in a heap. Jazz reached over and impulsively hugged me.

Dad was right, her hair smelled like Jazz's.

A couple of seconds passed. I couldn't bring myself to hug her back, so as I scrambled to my feet, I extended my hand. "Here, let me help you up."

"You do it for everyone else," Jazz said. She took my hand and tugged herself up. "It'll be better now, Sunn. I'm here to help."

I'd never felt this connected, never felt anything like affection for my sister. I was getting confused. This was the sister I'd always wanted. Mom accepted her as her daughter, why couldn't I just take her as my sister? Let her help me carry the load that was our family.

Because she wasn't real. Not the real Jazz anyway.

"Hey, take your bath before we have to build an ark," I said. "I'll unpack your bag for you."

"Already did. But hang here in my room. We need a battle plan for whipping this family into shape." She curtseyed like a servant to the queen. "Now, I can't let a good bath go to waste." She stepped back and closed the door.

I wandered to the bed and sat. Surveying the room, I toted up the differences. Mom hadn't touched this room since Jazz left. It had been a shrine to her disorder. Jazz dropped things as she shed them, waiting for them to disappear, then reappear washed, hung, folded by magic. The parts of the room this girl had touched were military in their tidiness. The comb and brush lay aligned on the dresser. The pictures on the dresser were straightened, and the top dusted. A novel with a bookmark sticking out an orderly inch resided on the nightstand, and the edges of the book squared with the table corner.

I rose and went to the closet. The bifold doors were closed neatly. Wrong again. Opening the doors, I saw the clothes hung regimentally, shoulders adjusted neatly on the hangers, hangers spaced evenly, and the shoes ranked on the floor like foot soldiers on parade.

I found the carpetbag suitcase. Empty. Cleared completely, stored away in the back corner of the closet. Moving back to the bed, I opened the nightstand drawer. It held a black leather wallet placed neatly in one corner, a travel-size container of facial tissue next to it, and beneath them, a book that looked like an oversized diary.

Snagging the wallet, I flipped it open to the driver's license. Not-Jazz's picture smiled from a New York license with Jazz's name, hair and eye color, weight, and a New York address. Placed neatly in the pockets were a Visa and a social security card, each in Jazz's name. The social security card was old and wrinkled. I had little doubt that the number was Jazz's. This girl had been too careful to leave anything to chance.

I was reaching for the big diary when I heard the tub draining. I slid the drawer shut. This would have to wait. I sat back on the bed and lounged in studied nonchalance.

Chapter Ten

Whendalf Jazz stepped out of the bathroom, she wore one towel wrapped around her body, and with another, she dried her hair.

"That was great. Our New York apartment only had a shower I had to wedge myself into. Vermont had communal showers. I haven't had a luxurious soak since I left home."

She pulled the towel away and ruffled her hair with her fingers. "Thanks, Sunn, I feel like a whole new person."

I smiled. No kidding. "I'm full of good ideas." I rolled off the bed and stood. "We never got to the brownies at dinner. I'll make some iced tea. Talking about this family's problems needs strong measures."

"Chocolate, the wonder drug." Jazz snapped the towel at me. "My sister, the genius."

Dodging the snapping towel, I dashed out. As I skipped down the stairs, I realized I was smiling.

I cut the brownies and arranged them on a plate. I popped the fudge ripple ice cream into the microwave, nuked it for twenty seconds to soften, and poured the tea. Plopping the carton of ice cream in the middle of the kitchen table, I stabbed two spoons into it and put two shallow bowls on the table. One had a picture of Pooh in the bottom, and the other sported Eeyore. The bowls had been our ice cream bowls since we were tots. I thought I'd see how much Reynolds lore this girl had accumulated. I put the tea glasses next to the bowls, then, as an after-thought, broke off two sprigs of mint from the flowerpot on the sill and dropped one into each glass.

Jazz appeared in the kitchen. She wore the same jeans but a different tee. "Be still, my beating heart—fudge rip-ple." She grinned at me. "I think that I'm about to gain my weight back." She dragged out a chair and reached for a bowl. Eeyore. Wrong.

She plunked a brownie into the bowl, scooped ice cream on top, and dug in. "Fortified with brownie and fudge ripple, we can fix a crack in the world." She took a sip of tea, wrinkled her nose, then, with thumb and forefinger, tweezed out the mint and slid it onto the rim of her bowl.

When this girl failed the Jazz test, I was momentarily sad.

"There's old Toulouse." Jazz popped up from her chair and went to the refrigerator. "Still the vulture of the fridge, hey, Toulouse?" She scrubbed the cat's ears and scratched under his chin. "How you doin', guy? I know you missed me."

Toulouse purred and twitched his tail. Rolling over to expose his belly, he swatted at Jazz's fingers.

"Oh, I get an 'upside down' huh? You must have missed me a lot." She rubbed the cat's stomach. "Sorry, Toulouse, the ice cream's a meltin'. I'll let you lick the bowl."

She returned to her bowl and took another bite. "I told Rhonda and her boyfriend, Emory, about Toulouse. They thought it was hilarious that he's always on top of the fridge. We even made up a short scene for our acting class with Toulouse in it. We had this girl arguing with her boyfriend. She compares him to her roommate's cat. The cat wants to be petted, but won't let anyone hold him. It was a cool scene."

And then I knew how this girl had pulled it off. I had to find the diary in Jazz's nightstand drawer.

"Tell me about Rhonda. And Emory. What kind of name is 'Emory'?" I asked.

"Rhonda and I met at acting class. She moved in with

me because I needed someone to share expenses. She was dating Emory. He modeled some. He was a Nordic god. Blond, blue-eyed, and totally gorgeous. Rhonda talked him into joining our acting class."

Jazz took another brownie, slathered it with more ice cream, and went on.

"I teased him a lot about his name. I thought it was made up. Emory Emerson, *puh-lease*. I told him that he sounded like a character in one of those tacky Southern romance novels. He swore his name was real, and that his background was more Trailer Park Gothic than Southern decadence. He was a terrific actor."

"Yeah? How's that?" I asked.

"Geez, he kind of 'became' people, you know?" Jazz gestured with her spoon. "He could meet somebody on the street, chat for a minute or two, then walk away and 'be' him. It even showed in his modeling portfolio. In one picture he's a tough hoodlum, sneering and dangerous, and in the next he's Ralph Lauren WASP, icy cool and unattainable."

"Sounds like you liked him," I said.

Jazz took another bite. She wrinkled her brow in thought as she chewed and swallowed. Then she tapped her spoon against the rim of her bowl. "You know what? I did. At first, Rhonda was happy that Emory and I got along so great, but then she got . . . I don't know . . . snarky about it."

"Jealous?"

"I guess. I told you that we hadn't been getting along and that's why I took the rep job. Traveling companies aren't the best gigs in the world. Keeps you out of touch with the good auditions in the city. But it was a little too tense around the place."

She turned her attention to her ice cream.

"What happened to Emory?" I asked.

Jazz put down her spoon. "I think he died in the fire." Her voice was whisper soft. "When I got back to New York and found our building burned, I called his place. The landlady told me that he'd moved. I asked her when he left, and it was the same week I hit the highway. When I talked to the police, I told them about Emory. They're going to check, see if anyone has heard from him."

She picked up her spoon, but tapped it aimlessly against the tea glass. "Guess Rhonda was planning to shove me out of the apartment when I got back."

I nodded, but didn't look at Jazz. The hamster was running in the wheel and I could barely keep up.

"So, enough about the not-quite-dead Jazz. Tell me about what's been happening here. I kind of stayed out of touch since I . . . um. . . ." Jazz twitched the corner of her mouth into a wry, embarrassed smile.

"Defected?"

"Yeah, that about says it." Jazz shrugged.

I drew circles with my spoon in the brownie crumbs and melted ice cream at the bottom of my bowl. I let the silence deepen as I remembered Jazz's departure.

Jazz's graduation last May had been filled with pomp and circumstance. Mom had dessert for a family celebration waiting for us after the ceremony. After eating cake and accepting congratulations, Jazz went upstairs to change. She had plans to go to New Braunfels for a weekend fling of tubing and partying with friends. When her friends honked outside, Jazz skipped down the stairs with a bulging duffel, waved a cheery good-bye, and left.

And didn't come back. A long letter on yellow stationery propped against a pillow on her unmade bed told us Jazz was going to New York. She would be an actress. Because she was eighteen, they couldn't make her come home. She wished she hadn't had to deceive them, but she knew Mom and Dad would have tried to keep her with them. Promising to write and call, she hoped they would understand that she couldn't give them her address or phone number.

There was more, paragraph upon paragraph about Jazz's need to be free, to spread her wings, et cetera, et cetera, et cetera.

I thought the letter was vintage Jazz, self-absorbed and bereft of consideration for our parents' anguish.

Mom and Dad were blindsided. They had never seen this Jazz. As long as Jazz needed them, she manipulated them with her charm. Now they were expendable, and she left them behind like a bad debt. Mom blamed Dad's drinking, Dad blamed Mom's neediness, and both, I think, blamed me because I was always a convenient target. Nobody blamed Jazz.

Not-Jazz interrupted my thoughts. "Sunn, I admit it. It was a kind of treason. But call me some real bad names and get past it. I know Dad left soon after I did, but Mom didn't make much sense when she told me about it."

I nodded. "Yeah, you called in . . . what . . . August?"

Jazz shrugged again. "I guess."

I could tell she didn't have this information.

"With you gone, Mom and Dad lost the glue that stuck them together. He started drinking, big time, and she got worse."

"How could she get worse?"

I caught myself rubbing at my face, mirroring Dad's quirk. This girl didn't have a clue how bad it had gotten. But then, neither had the real Jazz.

"She didn't want anyone but Dad or me in the house.

Then she didn't want to be alone at night, and then she wouldn't answer the phone, get dressed, cook, clean, or sleep. If she was having a good day, I could get her to drive to the grocery store, but she wouldn't go without me. Every so often I could get her to church."

Jazz placed her hand on mine, stopping my spoon from scratching the bowl's bottom.

"You're gonna bend the spoon."

I jumped.

"Sorry," I said.

"No. I'm sorry." Jazz grinned like a silly wood imp. "*And I apologize.*"

I grinned back.

Jazz squeezed my hand, then let go. "I saw the wooden shutters were closed when I got here. Mom won't let you open them, will she?"

I shook my head.

Jazz got up and went to the refrigerator. She stroked Toulouse's back until he purred, a loud, coarse rasp.

"Maybe you'll get to be a kid again, now that I'm here to help," she said.

"I never was a kid, and besides, life's not a play, Jazz. You can't rewrite the past."

Jazz smiled a dreamy, faraway smile. "Sure you can, Sunny. Sure you can."

Chapter Eleven

"Jasmine?" Mom's voice drifted into the kitchen. She sounded frightened and lost, a child calling for her mother.

I looked at Jazz. "The pill shouldn't have worn off. Why don't you go reassure her you're still here? She ought to go back to sleep."

"Sure," Jazz said. "I'll sit with her. Will she want me to read to her or something?"

Suddenly I wanted to hurt this girl. Make her pay for Jazz's sin of selfishness. "Go look under my bed. Your old scrapbook is there. She looks at it for hours. She sits in a chair wearing a ratty old robe, her hair unwashed, looks at your scrapbook and cries. By the hour, by the day, by the week—"

Jazz cut me off. "I'm sorry. Sunn, how many times can I say it? I'm sorry. I . . . I didn't know."

"You didn't care." The words were out before I could stop them. Jazz sighed, and left.

I pushed my bowl away. The spoon clattered; the bowl hit the ice cream carton and tipped over. The rim rolled back and forth across the wooden table.

Stupid, I thought. She's. Not. Jazz.

The phone rang and I jumped. As my knees struck the table, the bowl rocked off the edge, clattered to the brick floor, and bounced. Pooh was safe. Plastic bowls for little kids, safe from accidents and temper tantrums.

Hooking the receiver on the second ring, I tucked it between my ear and shoulder. "Hello."

"Good, I was hoping you'd answer."

"Dad, you make it to dry land?"

"What's that crack supposed to mean?"

"Think about it, it'll come to you."

Dad's sigh was deep and disgusted. "Do you want to talk about this . . . "—he groped for words—"this situation, or do you want to make me the villain in your little melodrama?"

"Whatever. What do you need?"

"I'm going to call Ollie."

"The police chief? I thought you wanted to sort it out by ourselves," I said.

"Once I was away, I got to wondering what this girl's agenda could be."

I slid down in my chair and rested my head against the back. Dad had put some geography between himself and this girl's "Jazz-spell," and his reporter radar had kicked in.

"I want to find out if anyone wasn't there when the building burned. Someone that lived there. I think this girl knows Jazz and might have lived there or visited."

"I think I know who she might be."

"You do?"

"I drew her a nice hot bath, and while she was soaking, I snooped."

"Good work, Sunn. I always knew you had a criminal streak."

"She has a New York driver's license with her picture, Jazz's name, address, weight, hair color, the works. She also has what looks like Jazz's social security card and a Visa in her name."

Silence from the receiver.

"Dad?"

"Just processing the info. My guess is the credit card and social security card are Jazz's. Easy to steal. But the driver's license would take a little more work."

"I guess Jazz might have gotten a driver's license, but how'd this girl's picture get on it?"

"Maybe I'll have Ollie check it out."

Nobody said anything for a few seconds.

"I know something else," I said.

"What?"

"She mentioned her roommate and the roommate's boyfriend. She said she told them stories about Toulouse."

"Toulouse? What about the fur ball?" Dad sounded impatient.

"She said they used Toulouse in a scene for acting class."

"Keep going."

"Dad." Now I was impatient. "Think. Jazz used stuff about us in scenes for class. So this girl must be her roommate."

"Could be." Dad's voice sounded deep in thought. "Or, someone in her class who saw the scenes."

"My bet is on the roommate. And there's a big book, like an oversized diary, in the nightstand with the wallet. I want to get a look at it."

"Good idea. Okay, that gives me a lot to go on."

I waited for thanks, but none came.

"Now, I don't want to talk on the phone. Inquiring ears and all that. E-mail me anything else you find. And activate the disk lock system, or delete your posts and empty the trash."

He hesitated a minute. "Sunny, give me your gut feeling. Is this girl dangerous? Are you and Lily safe?"

I thought. "I'm not scared. Curious, but not scared. And I think we'll do Mom more harm making this girl go than letting her stay. At least until we know what's going on."

"For the life of me, I don't know why, but I don't want to tell anyone about her yet. I'll call Ollie and get him to check out the roommate." Beard-scrubbing noises. "I've warted him so much before, he'll just think it's more of the same." We didn't speak for a long minute. I remembered Dad's late-night calls to Ollie, full of drunken babbling and conspiracy theories. Dad cleared his throat. "You try to get to that book. But don't take any chances."

"Gee, Dad, I didn't know you cared," I said.

"You'd have a smart remark for Mother Teresa." He hung up.

I got up and slammed the receiver onto the base.

I grabbed the ice cream, slapped on the lid, jerked open the freezer door, pitched in the carton, and slammed the door. Toulouse curled his tail around his body and shot me a murderous look.

"If I wanted to slam your tail in the door, you'd already be howling." I trudged upstairs, leaving the dirty bowls on the table.

Chapter Twelve

As I climbed the stairs, I heard gentle murmurs of conversation drift from Mom's room. I slipped quietly down the hall, stopping outside the open door.

"Mom, Sunny's been here helping you, and it's like you don't even see her. Dad's the same way. Why do you treat her that way?"

Mom's answer was wistful and a bit pleading. "Oh, Jazz, Sunny doesn't want us to treat her any other way. She keeps herself apart, closed off. She was even a disagreeable baby."

I closed my eyes.

"Mom, all babies are sweet."

I heard the bedsprings creak.

"Jazz, honey, it's a long, complicated story."

"I'm not going anywhere, Mom."

I moved closer to the door.

Mom's voice was soft and sad when she began talking. "When you were born, we lived in New York. The Village. Your father loved his job, and we were happy. But the year you were five, several things happened at once."

"What?" Jazz asked.

I leaned against the wall. This girl wasn't good; she was terrific. By nightfall, she'd know enough Reynolds family history to go on a game show.

"I was mugged at the park. I used to take you in a red wooden-sided wagon, remember?"

Jazz's voice sounded like a smile would. "Sure do."

"The man ran up and grabbed my purse. When he yanked it, I was knocked off-balance. I fell onto the wagon and knocked you out onto the sidewalk. You broke three fingers, and I broke my ankle." Mom paused. "I got hysterical, I guess. I was four months' pregnant, and I was afraid I'd lose the baby."

I heard gentle, comforting sounds from Jazz.

"We were splinted and bandaged and painted with Mercurochrome. But bandages didn't fix everything. I didn't want to stay in New York. I wasn't a city mouse. Just a mouse." Mom sighed. It sounded like a punctured tire. "Of course, I'd never liked New York. Was uneasy with all the bustle. But I needed an excuse, and I guess I found one. Or it found me."

"Don't worry about it, Mom. Go on with the story."

"Then out of nowhere, Momma and Dad had great luck. They leased some of our land to an oil company and it hit. They were rich. Dad decided he wanted to live someplace that wasn't Texas. Since Momma would never sell this old place, she gave it to me."

I knew most of the rest. Mom gave Dad an ultimatum. He could stay in New York alone or in Texas with her and Jazz. He came, but he hated it. And I was born. The polar opposite of Jazz. Jazz, who slept like an angel, ate anything, born smiling.

I tuned back in to their conversation when I heard Mom sigh again.

"But Sunny was born with her fists clenched. She had colic until she was eight months old, and then she was teething. She didn't cry, she howled. She never slept, and she spit out her food. The only thing she liked was her bath. It was the only time she didn't scream."

Mom laughed, low and rueful. "At least she was always clean. I don't know how many times I bathed that child in a single day.

"Dan started going to the bars, drinking, but his columns were still good. When he'd come home, Sunny was screaming, I was crying, and you—you were happy to see him."

"What was wrong with Sunny?"

Mom began to cry. "I believe she absorbed all the unhappiness in our house. Just soaked it in. When she learned to talk, she used words to fight back."

There was a long silence. "I think Dan is a little frightened of Sunny. She's the only one in this family that can hold her ground. And I'm. . . ." She paused. "I'm sad that Sunny's so angry, but I don't know how to help her. And I'm too tired to try."

I had heard all I needed about my faults and shortcomings. I backed a few steps down the hall and turned into the fourth bedroom—Dad's study. I closed the door and sat in the leather desk chair facing the computer.

The idea of Dad being frightened of me was interesting. Dad and I had connected in only one way. Curiosity. He called me a seeker. I questioned everything. If Mom called the couch camel-backed, I wanted to know why. Dad had even directed my reading early on. My fascination with Leonardo da Vinci came from him. While Mom did most of the cooking, Dad did the occasional gourmet thing, telling me that Leonardo believed we should seek and master all facets of life—and cooking was a creative art. He even showed me the mirror-writing. And I used it to keep Jazz from reading the journals I kept. Dad taught me to use the computer, showed me how to do research, then hated it when I used my knowledge to argue with him.

Thinking for a moment, I reached across to the computer and punched the buttons. As the computer booted, I drummed my fingertips on the keyboard.

I clicked the icon for the Internet service, typed in my password, and waited. The computer ticked, whirred, and made the dialing tones. When the logo filled the screen, I slid the mouse and clicked the mail icon.

Once the blank form for messages came up, I began typing.

Send to: rocketman@tol.com

Re: names

Message: Forgot to give names. Roommate Rhonda, didn't get last name. Rhonda's boyfriend Emory Emerson. J thinks guy died in fire. Said maybe moved in with Rhonda while J touring. Says she told the NY police about him. U check?

Clicking the send icon, I waited until the screen flashed the sentence, Your mail has been sent. I deleted my post from the archives, emptied the trash, exited the program, shut down the system, and turned off the computer.

Propping my elbows on the desk, I put my head on my hands, palms nested into eye sockets. I rubbed my palms against my closed eyes. Why was I so tired? Is this how Mom feels?

I rolled the chair away from the desk and stood. I might not know which way to turn, but I knew the way to Jazz's room, and I was going to get that diary.

Easing the door open, I paused. I heard Jazz and Mom talking. Snatches of the conversation were just loud enough for me to know they were looking at the scrapbook. I whisked across the hall and through Jazz's open door. Moving purposefully, I crossed the braided rug. Reaching the nightstand, I ran my palms along the sides of my legs, drying them on the denim overalls. My hand trembled as I placed it on the drawer knob, then pulled.

"Sunny."

I turned, my heart galloping.

The girl who was not Jazz stood in the doorway, one hand on her hip. Her face was not open and welcoming now. Her eyes were slits of calculation and suspicion. "Is there something you need?"

I stood, frightened and mute.

"Fine, don't answer." The girl moved toward me, coming closer with each step. "I know what you came here to steal."

Chapter Thirteen

I flinched as Jazz reached past me and pointed to the open drawer.

"Go ahead, look," Jazz commanded.

Turning, I looked into the drawer.

"See, it's not there." Jazz put both hands on her hips. "I can't believe you're still doing this."

The drawer was as it had been earlier. The wallet, the tissues, and the journal were still smartly aligned.

"I guess I'm a big disappointment." Jazz flopped onto the bed.

I resumed breathing, but had no idea what to say.

"Sorry, kiddo, but I barely had enough money in New

York for cereal and milk. I had to give up the Snickers habit." Jazz sprawled against the pillows. She propped one ankle on the other knee, slipped her shoe off the heel, and swung it back and forth on her toes.

"Geez, Karen, I'd almost forgotten your Snickers raids."

The gears in my stalled mind jammed. *Karen?* I stared at Jazz.

While Jazz's body was relaxed, her expression was intense. She watched her shoe sway faster on her twitching toes. But I don't think she saw a shoe.

"I don't—"I began.

"Oh, boo, you certainly do. I always had my emergency Snickers hidden in my nightstand, and you used to snitch it. You knew I wouldn't tell, since Mom thought chocolate was a deadly poison."

Jazz blinked then, and confusion clouded her eyes. She grabbed the shoe, sat up, and placed it carefully onto her foot. She looked at me, her eyes again open and welcoming. "Right?"

"Right."

"Great." Jazz stood up. I backed away.

"While Mom's asleep, I'll rustle up a light supper. Why don't you relax or read or something? You look tired."

"Yeah, thanks." I turned and escaped.

I entered my room, overwhelmed with relief. After that last exchange, I wouldn't have been overly surprised to find the furniture on the ceiling or grass growing on the walls.

I sat down in the wooden rocking chair. Running my right hand along the curved arm, I felt comforted by its familiarity. I had painted this chair myself.

When we were younger, Jazz and I weren't allowed to play in our house's huge attic. But I, of course, had to prowl its corners and recesses. I found the battered rocking chair, hauled it down, stripped it, and painted it white. I settled it in my room and installed the then-kitten Toulouse as king.

When Mom saw the chair, her lips thinned. "I used to rock Jazz in that chair when she was a baby. But you seemed to hate it, so I put it away," she said. From then on, when I was upset, Toulouse and I rocked ourselves into calm. As the cat got older, he preferred the terra firma of the refrigerator, but would haul his fuzzy butt upstairs when he heard the chair's runners slap against the wooden-plank floor. I rocked now. Thinking. Toulouse appeared, jumped into my lap, kneaded his paws into my shoulder, and head-butted my chin. I scratched and buffed the cat absently.

Karen. Who was *Karen?* And what was that stuff about chocolate? We'd just eaten brownies and fudge ripple ice cream. And Snickers raids?

My rocking accelerated with my confusion. Jazz seemed different when she called me Karen. Her face changed, as if some unseen artist had pressed and pushed the soft clay of a sculpted head. Her whole demeanor was different. Not-Jazz lost her Jazz persona.

I shook my head. This was getting out of hand. A snatch of conversation shouldered its way into my thoughts. When Jazz spoke of Emory, she said he could "become" other people. It was obvious this girl had "become" Jazz. But she called me Karen. Did Rhonda know Karen? Or— the skin on my arms prickled—"goose walked over your grave" Granny used to call the feeling—had she done this before? If she could become Jazz, couldn't she have become someone else? Was she getting her cast of characters confused? Who *was* this girl?

And where was Jazz? Had she died in the fire? Or had she instructed this girl and sent her here?

Why would Jazz do that?

As I calmed, the rocking slowed. I had to get a look at the journal, and Dad had to get some information on Jazz's roommate.

I stilled the chair. The words of some snappy song drifted up the stairs. Jazz was singing in the kitchen, absorbed with her Becky Home-Ecky imitation. Standing, I whispered, "Time's a-wastin'."

I went down the hall and into Jazz's room. I whipped across the floor and pulled the drawer handle. The drawer opened easily. The wallet and the box of tissues were there. But that was all.

The journal was missing.

Chapter fourteen

I picked up the wallet and the tissues, as if removing them would make the journal reappear. The faded shelf paper, white background with yellow flowers, jasmine, of course, was all that was left in the drawer.

She had moved it. She knew I wasn't jonesing for a Snickers, but she couldn't admit she's a fake.

The phone shrilled and my heart clutched. I heard Jazz answer. I willed my feet to move, and slipped into the bathroom. I ran water in the sink and splashed it on my face. I was wiping my face on a hand towel when I heard Jazz coming up the stairs.

"Sunn?"

"Yeah, in here."

Jazz appeared at the door. "Dad wants to talk to you."

"Okay," I said, hanging the towel on the rack. "I'll get it in Dad's study."

Jazz seemed tense. "Something you don't want me to hear?"

I didn't answer.

Jazz's eyes darkened. "That's the way you want to play this?"

She held my gaze for a couple of seconds, then turned and stamped down the stairs without another word or a backward glance.

I went to the study and picked up the extension. "Okay, Jazz, you can hang up."

"Sure. Dad, when will I see you again?" Jazz asked.

"I'll probably come by tomorrow," Dad replied.

"Visit your prodigal child?" Jazz asked.

"You bet," Dad said. I thought that lighthearted answer sounded a bit too lighthearted. Forced.

"Great, I'll see you then." I heard Jazz hang up her extension.

"Sunny?"

"Yeah, Dad. I was waiting for her to hang up."

"I've got some news. Go get online," Dad said.

"Sure." I put the phone in its cradle and punched the

computer into life. As soon as I got connected, my screen had an instant message.

U there?

Here. I typed back. Got news 2.

You 1st.

Got into her room. She caught me B4 I got the journal.

And?

Weirdness. Called me Karen. Accused me of old habit stealing candy. Something about Mom said chocolate = poison.

No words appeared on the screen for almost a minute. I pictured Dad scrubbing at his face, deep in his ponder mode.

Like Alice said, getting curiouser and curiouser.

More. I typed. Journal gone.

Probably still in room. Def in house. Has she left?

Nope.

Important to find.

Right. Your news? I typed.

Hang on, if she moved journal

I was already typing. Doesn't want me to read. Must have info.

Again the screen remained static.

What U find out? I typed.

Called Ollie. Roommate Rhonda Mallory. Problem. NYPD called next of kin. Rhonda Mallory couldn't have been J's roommate.

I waited for more words to blip onto my screen. Finally they did.

Rhonda Mallory died. 5 yrz ago.

Chapter Fifteen

I stared at the screen. The words didn't change. My mind tumbling, I flexed my fingers over the keys, trying to make sense of this new scrap of information.

I typed, What's with all these dead girls that won't stay dead?

I hit the send icon. The screen seemed to stare at me, then a message flashed.

ROCKETMAN HAS DISCONNECTED.

Why would he do that, maybe he. . . .

Suddenly realizing what my last post said, I pulled my fingers away from the keyboard, as if it were infectious. I slumped back in the chair. Why do I do this shit?

I typed an e-mail that Dad would find the next time he booted up. I wish I weren't such a spiteful brat.

I looked at the message, wondering if it was true. I tapped the button, sending the message into cyberspace.

I trudged to my room and crashed onto my bed. I felt as if there were snakes in my head. If I opened my mouth, I would hiss.

I had to concentrate. The answer was simple. Jazz's roommate was another Rhonda Mallory. How many could there be in the world? The name wasn't an unusual one, like Gamma Ray or Ziggy Pumpkin or Leroy Pharts. I knew two Rhondas at school. True, none with the last name Mallory, but if I came up with two Rhondas in Podunk, Texas, some law of mathematics should ensure that more than one Rhonda in the entire United States would link up with Mallory.

I needed to ask a few questions, and Dad was probably fueling his anger with bourbon right about now. Whatever, he wasn't going to talk to me. I did my Leonardo da Vinci think-stream. Dad got the info from Ollie. Sunday. Dad said Ollie was at home. I didn't have to write backward to see the answer. Ollie knew me and knew Mom didn't have both oars in the water. He had actually let me bail Dad out for drunk-and-disorderly once. He'd help if he could.

Scrambling off the bed, I darted across the hall to the

study. I eased the door closed and flipped the latch. Perching on the edge of the chair, I yanked open the bottom drawer, pulled out the phone book, and plopped it on the desktop. I ran my fingers down the page, then dialed his home number. The phone was jerked up before the first ring was complete.

"'Lo."

The voice was a girl's.

"Laura?"

"Yeah, who's this?"

"It's Sunny Reynolds. Is your dad home?"

"On Sunday? With golf on the tube? Does the sun come up in the east?"

"Can I talk to him?"

"I guess, if I lead him here with a cold beer under his nose. Hold on."

Laura yelled for her dad, and I wondered if the windows in Ollie's house were shatterproof.

After some shuffling noise, Ollie said hello.

I heard Laura in the background: "And Dad, don't tie up the phone. I'm waiting for a call."

"Hello," Ollie repeated.

"Hello, Mr. Gains, it's Sunny Reynolds."

"Hey, Sunny, I just talked to your father."

"I know, but I need to ask you a couple of questions."

"Shoot."

"Dad said Rhonda Mallory has been dead for a while."

"Yup, that's what NYPD tells me."

"Surely there could be more than one Rhonda Mallory in the world?"

"Sunny, I told your dad all this."

"I know, but he's kind of not talking to me right now."

"We need to get Dan in AA."

"I know, Ollie, but right now, could we talk about the Rhonda Mallory thing?"

"Sure, there's probably a bushel basket full of Rhonda Mallorys, but this one has the same social security number, DOB, and place of birth as the one who attended Jazz's acting class. And those numbers match a death certificate for a girl that's buried in a little town in Maryland called Dobbins Bend."

I pulled in a deep breath. "How?"

"Let's just say if somebody wants to get real lost, they can become another person, if the other person happens to be resting in a cemetery plot. It's not as easy to do as it used to be, but it can get done. And as long as the person who wants to get lost doesn't file for benefits, she can hide for a long time behind a dead guy's identity."

I was silent. Finally I said, "Oh."

"Yup, the NYPD was gosh-awful interested in my call. I doubt your dad wants your mom to know, but I think those big-city cops think the apartment fire was hinky."

"Hinky?"

"Suspicious. They had already checked out Rhonda Mallory. She wasn't on the lease, but neighbors knew she lived there. They didn't want to give me any more information, but they wanted some from me. That tells me the case is open, and if it's still open, it's not listed as an accident."

When I didn't answer, Ollie asked, "You understand what I'm telling you?"

My voice shook. "Somebody set the fire, and Jazz wasn't killed in an accident. She was murdered."

"Yeah, that's the way I'm reading it. My call with the Mallory name practically made the lead detective shit and fall back in it."

"Did they follow it up?"

"The big boys don't share with their country cousins if they don't have to. But like I said, they had run her through the computer before and got a hit on a dead Rhonda Mallory."

"In Dobbins Bend."

"Maryland. Yeah."

"Did they talk to anyone about her?"

"Didn't tell me. It's really not my case; it's New York's. I told Dan what I got and suggested he talk to the city boys himself."

"Thanks, Ollie."

"If you call New York, talk to Detective Morino. Your dad might not have gotten to it yet, if you know what I mean."

"I'll do that."

"Sunny, I told your father. None of this makes much difference. This Rhonda Mallory might not be who she says she is—but it doesn't have much to do with you. If we find out she was responsible for that fire, then we can deal with that. But keeping this thing stirred up isn't going to help your family. Jazz is dead, and this Rhonda is New York's problem."

I needed to think, so I didn't tell Ollie that Rhonda was very much our problem now.

I hung up and worked my jaw back and forth, trying to ease the tension. Things were weirder than ever.

Jazz wasn't really Jazz.

Rhonda wasn't really Rhonda.

And who the devil was Karen?

Chapter Sixteen

The sharp knock startled me.

"Sunn, you still on the phone?"

I rose slowly, unlocked the door, and stepped into the hall.

Not-Jazz looked at me, her expression tight and guarded. Distrustful. "Locking yourself in? Keeping secrets?"

That lit my fuse. I returned the look with a mirror image. We were like stray cats, mincing on restless paws, heads low.

"No more secrets than you," I said.

I saw her register my suspicion. All the smiles and hugs and fake affection fled from her in a flicker.

We had become opponents.

Jazz's eyes remained locked on mine. Her tone was even. "It's after six. We should wake Mom for dinner."

I took a step toward Jazz, a step of calculated dominance. "I'll go get her up. I try to keep her on some sort of schedule."

Jazz held her ground and her gaze. "You sound like you're taking care of a baby."

I recognized we were in a war of wills. With Jazz, that had been familiar ground.

"It's a lot like that," I said, my tone taking on brittle edges.

"Maybe she's an infant because you want her to be. You aren't happy unless you're bossing Mom around. Is that the only way you can feel important?"

"That's sweet, Jazz. You dump the problem in my lap, and now you spout New Age psycho-voodoo at me. You remind me of Dad."

"Like father like daughter, right, Sunny?"

I stepped back. The contest was over. Jazz won. Because I spoke to this false Jazz as if she were the real one. This girl morphed into a clone of Jazz's shadow self, the Jazz who didn't charm. The Jazz I had known.

"Fine," I said, dropping my gaze. I turned as I spoke, tossing the words over my shoulder. "Do what you want."

I trudged to the kitchen. The table was set for three. Bright place mats, deliberately mismatched dishes. That was right. Jazz hated things that came in a set. She used pieces of different sets, coordinated chaos, definitely a Jazz trademark.

I sat at my usual place and waited, drumming my fingertips against the oak surface.

Jazz pushed the door open and guided Mom in.

Mom pressed her hands together. "Oh, Lord, look at all the mixed-up dishes. The table hasn't looked like this since Jazz left." Tears gathered in her eyes; then her eyes widened. "I mean, since you've been gone." Mom sounded guilty of something. "I've gotten used to speaking of you as if you weren't here."

Jazz kissed Mom's cheek. "I understand, Mom. Let's relax and enjoy the salad." She settled Mom into a chair and took her own.

"You know, when I was in New York, I went to the Saturday-morning flea markets, bought one dish here, a cup there, and a saucer someplace else. Not one piece of tableware matched another. And every place mat was a different color or pattern."

Mom sighed. "I could never do that. I'd feel like Momma would swoop down and send me straight to my room. You didn't break rules around Momma. And matching dishes was a sacred rule." She smiled as Jazz tossed the salad. She held up her plate so Jazz could fill it.

Jazz heaped spinach salad onto her own plate, then released the tongs. I tensed my jaw at the deliberate slight, and served myself. "I remember. In fact, I told my roommate about her."

Jazz giggled and poured tea. "My roommate couldn't believe Granny was so judgmental over such little things."

"She judged everyone and found them all lacking," Mom said. "Except you, Jasmine. She thought anything you did was charming."

"But Sunny's more like her," Not-Jazz said.

Real Jazz was always subtle. She didn't kill you with the arrow, but with the infection it caused.

"Granny Wilson is the sanest person in this family," I said. Outright warfare had always been my character trait.

"She's mean to Mom," Jazz said. "She moved before you could really see that." Jazz poured her own tea, after filling Mom's glass, then turned and poured mine. She gave me a tight, condescending smile.

This girl could make me feel useless, stupid, and unwanted just like Jazz could, but she was not my sister.

I slapped my fork down. I had to get to the bottom of this. When I looked up, Jazz and Mom were staring at me.

"Whatever is the matter with you, Sunny?" Mom's voice was disapproving.

"Nothing. I mean, I remembered something I have to do before it gets too late."

"What might that be?" Jazz asked.

"I, uh . . ." I tried to summon a reasonable excuse to keep Jazz's suspicion at bay.

"I thought, I'd . . ." and inspiration struck. "I think I'll skip school tomorrow. I want to spend more time with you. We're doing reviews for exams, and I'm exempt. One of the perks of no social life—good grades." Jazz might not be fooled, but she wouldn't make a scene in front of Mom.

"I'll call Ms. Collins and tell her why I won't be there."

Mom dropped her fork. "Don't!" Mom clutched my wrist, as if to physically keep me from the phone.

"Mom?" I made my voice calm, trying to soothe her.

"Goodness." Mom released my arm and worked at a smile. "I didn't mean to shout, dear. I just don't want you to tell anyone Jazz is home."

"Why not, Mom?" Still trying to calm my mother, I kept my questions soft-edged.

"I'd like to have Jazz to myself for a little while. Once you tell Myra Collins, it'll be all over town. The phone will ring off the hook, and the front door will need new hinges with everybody running here to see Jasmine." She paused, then said, almost under her breath, "Sunny, you know how everyone loved Jazz."

There it was again. Mom speaking of Jazz in the past tense—and as if she weren't in the room.

"Oh," I said. "Sure, I didn't think. I'm not used to people coming by and calling anymore."

"Jazz had so many friends."

I backed up. "I'll tell Ms. Collins I'm sick and won't be at school. If I don't tell them I'm going to be absent, they'll call Dad. If they can't get him, Mr. Preston might come by to check on us."

"The principal?" Jazz was incredulous.

My response was quick and sharp. "Jazz, the entire town knows our family's sad story. We're the Mad Hatters of this little Wonderland. If I don't show and don't call, the vultures get a whiff of roadkill and start circling."

"Sunny!" Mom was white and shaking. "Don't speak about us like that. Don't ever speak about us like that, do you hear me?"

"I hear you," I said. I bolted from the room and tore up the stairs. I heard Mom say "us." And *us* didn't include me.

Chapter Seventeen

I stormed to my room and slammed the door. I slung myself into the rocker. I couldn't do what Dad wanted. I had to confront this girl and send her away. When the real Jazz left for New York, I knew my place in the world for the first time ever. I was the key player, captain of the team, leader of the pack.

I cooled myself out a bit. And decided. There was something I had to do, and I didn't care if Not-Jazz caught me. This game of pretending not to be a cat while Not-Jazz pretended not to be a mouse was demented. The rest of the family might be running a bit short on sanity, but I wasn't.

I took a deep, satisfying breath and rubbed my palms

against my legs. I strode resolutely through the bathroom and into Jazz's room. Like a heat-seeking missile, I went to the closet, swung open the door, and knelt next to the suitcase. I unzipped it and pulled it open as I tugged it closer to the light and me. The journal was there, just as I knew it would be.

Tucking it against my chest, I rose, leaving the suitcase gaping open, the closet door ajar. This stranger might have something to hide, but I didn't.

I returned to my room, leaving the connecting doors open, daring Jazz to confront me. Flopping on the bed, I wadded the pillow to prop my head and support my neck. Picking up the book, I slid my thumb down the edge and opened it to the first page.

This journal is an assignment. Acting is a lot like therapy, I think. We have to analyze ourselves. Write our "backstory." Find our underlying motivations. Analyze our most important relationships. If we can do it for our own lives, we will be able to do it for a role.

The next page was blank with the exception of a few words in the center: "JAZZ ESCAPES THE COCOON AND BECOMES A BUTTERFLY." I turned the page and began reading.

"Cocoon" is really not the word I should use to describe my life until now. It was more of a prison. A prison run by benevolent wardens. Sound strange? Try to live it.

My parents love me, in fact, they adore me, and that's the problem. Both of them live through me, and I've known for some time they would never let me go. They can't let themselves see they've put the burden of their unhappiness square on my shoulders. I'm supposed to make them happy. And I've done it, I've been charming and pretty and smart and loving. But their need is a pit, and I can't fill it without throwing myself in.

I knew telling them I wanted to leave would be no good. They would, of course, tell me to go, to live my dream, but their eyes would show their sadness. They would look like I had chosen to die and leave them to their sorrow. They would make me too guilty to leave. And if I did manage to leave, I know the phone calls and letters would begin. Dad telling me how depressed Mom was, Mom telling me how Dad was drinking more, both of them asking me to come home, just for a visit. Unless I cut the cord, that noose of love they put around my neck, then I might as well stay to become as sad and embittered as they are.

Sunny doesn't understand how good she's got it. She's so jealous because Mom and Dad ignore her. She's right; they can't see her. Somehow, Sunny evaded that noose when she was a baby. She's been like a porcupine since the day she was *born. And it was her salvation. She can leave, and they won't try to pull her back. No noose they can tighten. Sunny's free, and I've got to admit until now I've hated her for it.*

I paused. I'd had too many spins and whirls in the last two days. My balance was uncertain. I had vertigo of the emotions. As Grandpa Wilson always said, "You done bought the horse, now you gotta put him in the barn."

I began reading again.

It's some kind of deranged custom in our lunatic family to bestow girl children with flower names. Actually, it's more of a family curse. I think it's one of those self-fulfilling type things, where a person grows into the name. I am Jasmine. The yellow jasmine represents grace and elegance. The flower has an exotic perfume that intoxicates those near it. I can still hear Mom telling me that when I was a child. Eager to please, I became what Mom wanted, grace and elegance. It was easy. She saw what she wanted to see.

Sunny's name is really Sunflower. Poor kid, the name alone is awful. I mean, why not name her something equally stupid, like Tomato Paste or Motor Oil? To make it worse, the sunflower represents haughtiness. Mom must have been in a real snit when she picked that one. As Sunny grew older, Mom always told us the name must have been inspired, because Sunny always stood apart, like she was too good to mingle with the rest of us flowers. Hey, I'm living proof that if you tell a child something often enough, they will finally listen. I look at Sunny differently. I see her keeping her head turned toward the sun and rejecting the darkness. And the darkness is our family.

I had to stop reading.

Why, if Jazz felt this way about me, had she been so cruel? And whatever this journal said, the cruelty had been there.

I turned back to my sister's words.

Whatever the reason—her fault, weird DNA, nurture, or nature, whatever—Sunny's all sharp quills. I know it's defense, but you still can't get close. Sunny's always ready for hurt, almost welcoming it, so she can draw blood with those sharp bristles. Unless you're a saint, you turn away from things that hurt you. Or you hurt back. I did both.

I rationalize this by telling myself I made sure Sunny was free to go when she was ready. She frightens my parents with her hard edges. If Sunny hated us enough, even if I left Mom and Dad in Sunny's care, she would still escape from them when it was time. Sunny was taught by all of us to be that hard.

It's odd that I'm supposed to be writing my story, and I've spent most of the time writing about Sunny. And a thought just came to me. When Sunny looked at Mom, Dad, or me, we realized she saw all our failings. We were reflections, and Sunny was the mirror. You can't get through a mirror, and you can't like it for showing you the truth. I had to get away from that mirror as much as I had to slip the noose from around my neck.

And that's the story of Jazz's cocoon. I had to write it, had to see the words to understand it. The rest of the story will be of the new Jasmine. The Jasmine of my own invention.

Chapter Eighteen

T he rest of the page was blank.

I turned the page. The handwriting was hurried, more careless than the pages before. There was an assortment of notes, odd scraps, snatches of conversation, short physical descriptions, and pages of scenes, scenes for actors. There were dialogue, stage directions, bits of business for the actors to follow. And these miniplays told the story of our family. Mom's neediness, Dad's drinking, my plainness, Nasty's mean nature, Grandpa Wilson's quotable country platitudes. It was all there, a text detailing our history, quirks, and conversations. A curriculum for an impostor.

The journal told me how the girl had done it.

It didn't tell me why.

I rose, went to the study, and called Ms. Collins. I told her Mom and I had the stomach flu. I assured her I had things under control and would call again tomorrow with an update. Mission accomplished, I returned to my room and picked up the journal. I slapped it against my thigh as I tramped down the stairs. Jazz and Mom were in the living room, watching TV.

Crossing to the television, I punched it off.

"Sunny!" Mom looked both startled and annoyed.

Jazz glared as she watched the journal slap, slap, slapping against my leg.

I interrupted Mom's complaint. "Mom, Jazz and I need to talk. Alone. Sister stuff. Mind if I take her upstairs for a bit?"

Without waiting for an answer, I flipped the TV back on, turned to Jazz, and gestured toward the stairs with the journal. Jazz's eyes locked on the book's marbled cover. She closed her eyes slowly, and then opened them and froze me with a level stare. Shark eyes—the dark, dead eyes of a predator.

Jazz nodded. "Back in a bit, Mom. Gotta tell Sunny the facts of life, I guess."

Mom looked confused and lapsed back into her language of fragmented sentences. "Oh, yes, well, you girls— I mean, do you think?" She waved her hand in front of her face.

"Sunny, let's get to it," Jazz said, and sauntered past me up the stairs.

I followed Jazz into her bedroom. She slid onto the bed and made a production of stacking pillows and settling them under her head. Finally, she sighed and folded her hands across her body.

"Are we adding breaking and entering to this family's tacky resume?" She pointed lazily to the opened closet door and the gaping suitcase.

I tossed the journal onto the bed but said nothing.

Jazz made no move. Not so much as a glance at the book. "Interesting reading?"

"Don't do laps with me." I felt my face flush, then reached out and slammed the closet door. "Drop the act. The journal told me how you did it. I want to know why."

Jazz opened her mouth in a delicate Southern belle yawn of boredom, covering her lips, oh, so politely, with her right hand.

"Why what?" She returned her hand to its resting place. "Why did I keep a journal? If you read it, you know. Why did I write scenes about our family? Well . . ." She took a long, purposeful pause. "Sunny, darlin', an author I've always admired said something to the effect that a messed-up family is the best inheritance a writer could get. I thought that would hold for actors, too. We used those scenes in my acting class."

"Stop it." My head pounded in rhythm with my heart. I took a step toward her. "Stop it now and tell me the truth."

"The truth? The truth is all there in black-and-white. Well, blue-and-white, never did like black ink. Don't worry, the students in class didn't believe any one family could have that many crazies."

"You are not my sister." My voice was dead and cold.

"Sunny, Sunny. I know you wished me dead, but, little sister, like it or lump it, 'tis I."

"You aren't Jazz. Who are you? Why are you doing this?"

The girl rose, fluffed her hair, stretched languidly, and stepped abruptly toward me, too close, too fast. The eyes weren't dead now, they were animated with the excitement of the kill. Her voice, no longer satin, was low, sibilant, and dangerous as bared fangs.

"Get over yourself, Sunny. You're in denial. You don't want me back because it dumps you back down to being a bottom-feeder, struggling for the scraps I leave behind. But that's the way it is. I'm here to stay."

The girl stepped back, shrugged her body back into relaxed calm. She pasted on a smug three-cornered grin. "Ta, ta, darlin'." As she swept past me she said, "Got to get back. Mom can't seem to get along without me." She paused at the threshold and lounged against the door frame. "You know that, don't you, Sunn?"

I staggered into the bathroom, turned on the faucet, and splashed my face with cold water. Mom's words about my baby self being soothed by water drifted through my tumbling thoughts. Still the same old Sunny, always reaching for something outside myself for comfort. I stood up quickly and stared at my dripping face in the mirror. Snatching up a towel, I rubbed hard at my skin, drying it, punishing it, stirring it into action.

Discarding the towel and banging doors as I went, I marched across the hall and into the study and closed the door. I dialed, and told the operator that I needed directory assistance for Dobbins Bend, Maryland. I grimaced when I was told to have a good day, and grabbed a pencil when another perky voice asked how she could help.

"I need to find someone in Dobbins Bend. The last name is Mallory, but I don't know the first name. I'm looking for an old friend of mine, and her parents live there. Sorority reunion stuff, you know how it is." I could out-lie Jazz and Not-Jazz both, if I needed to.

"Sure, well, let's see . . . there's two Mallorys. Hey, you're in luck. One's a business, so this has to be the home number." Miss Perky recited the number and encouraged me to have a terrific reunion.

Without a pause, I dialed the new number. I steadied my voice while the phone rang.

"Hello." The voice was soft.

"Hello, is this the Mallory residence?"

"Yes, it is, but if this is a telephone solicitation—"

"It's not," I cut in. "I don't know exactly how to start this, but I need some information. It concerns my sister."

"Your sister? Do I know your sister?"

"I don't know, but"—I spoke in a rush—"do you know a Rhonda Mallory?"

The silence was long. I heard my heart pound in my ears.

"Before I continue talking, you'll have to tell me who you are and why you've called asking for information like this." The woman sounded calm, even gracious, but steel was in her quiet voice.

"My name is Sunny Reynolds. A girl named Rhonda Mallory is supposed to have roomed with my sister in New York last year. And I need to find her to ask her some questions."

Silence again.

When the woman spoke, her words were tinged with weariness. "When will this ever stop?" she said.

I didn't answer. The question wasn't for me.

I waited another long minute. "I'm doing this for my mother. There's a girl here pretending to be my sister—"

I heard the woman catch her breath. "All right. I don't like to talk about this, but I might know something about the situation you are in. And how your mother . . ." She trailed off.

"Thank you. Are you Rhonda Mallory's mother?"

"Yes and no. My daughter was Rhonda Mallory. She died five years ago. She was eighteen. She had leukemia."

"I'm sorry," I said.

"Yes, so am I. The New York police called me a few months ago asking about Rhonda. This is connected, isn't it?"

"I think so."

"I'll tell you what I told them. I believe a girl named Debra Hallard was your sister's roommate. She was using Rhonda's name."

"Do you know her?"

The woman's laugh was rueful. "Oh, I knew what she wanted me to know about her. When Rhonda was twelve, a girl moved in next door to us. A foster child. The Porters were deeply religious and childless. When Debra came, the Porters had three other foster children." The woman paused, but I remained silent. "Debra and Rhonda became friends. Close friends, almost like sisters."

Mrs. Mallory again stopped talking. "Sorry, but I have to have a cigarette. A truly disgusting habit, don't take it up, if you haven't already."

I heard a rustling sound. "Yes, I mean, no, I don't smoke. Don't plan to start."

I heard the woman exhale.

"Debra was charming, a lovely girl. When Rhonda got so frail, Debra came here and read to her, played quiet games. She didn't reject Rhonda, fearing her illness like other girls. Often she spent the night, because Rhonda was frightened of sleep. Did you know that's a common fear of the terminally ill?"

Again, I didn't answer. What could I say?

"Somehow, Debra was living here. Not going home at all. It was summer, no school. I was so grateful for the comfort she gave Rhonda, and it seemed natural she was here. The Porters, being the caring people they are, understood. They let her stay."

The woman took another deep drag on the cigarette. "And when Rhonda died"—her voice wavered, stopped, then continued—"when Rhonda died, Debra just . . . stayed. I wanted her here. That's a lie. I needed her here."

Another long silence, too long.

"Sorry, I drifted back," Mrs. Mallory said. "I'll skip the details. She stayed and soon began calling me Mom. She cut her hair. Rhonda had bangs until she lost her hair from the chemo, and Debra appeared at breakfast one morning with bangs."

I waited and guessed what the woman would say next.

"She started wearing Rhonda's clothes and using the little catchphrases Rhonda had. She referred to favorite foods of Rhonda's as being her own favorites. She'd say, 'Why don't you and I make a German chocolate cake—you know it's my favorite.' I asked the Porters to take her home, but Debra sobbed and cried. She went back to the Porters, but in the morning I'd find her in Rhonda's bed. She began calling herself Rhonda."

I was right. This girl "became" people. She became someone who had been lost, and went to parents made vulnerable by grief. Another thought occurred to me.

"Mrs. Mallory, describe Debra for me."

I heard the woman take another drag on the cigarette, then release the smoke in a sigh. "She was lovely. She had silky dark hair and thick, dark lashes that set off blue eyes. And the most soothing voice. I thought it was her best feature."

"Yes," I said. I knew that soothing voice, but I also knew the other one, the one that sounded like the hiss of a pit viper.

"Mrs. Mallory, I'm sure Debra is the girl we're both talking about. She arrived at our house saying she's my older sister, Jazz."

"Is . . . is your sister. . .?"

"Dead," I answered. "We think so. There was a fire in her New York apartment. It has taken some time to identify—"

The woman cut in. "I see. Your poor mother."

"Yes, and it would take too long to explain why she's still here, still pretending, but something she said . . ." I faltered.

"What did she say?" The woman sounded impatient.

"She called me Karen and talked about her mother refusing to let her eat chocolate. I know that sounds strange, but—"

"But you want to know if she's dangerous?" I heard her pull on her cigarette. "Yes, she certainly is."

Chapter Nineteen

rs. Mallory spoke a long time. Her story was part
fact and part supposition. Then I heard a slight
snick and an odd hollow sound, as if Mrs.
Mallory spoke from the bottom of a well. Mrs. Mallory
heard it also, and stopped speaking.

"Sunny, does your phone have an extension?"

"Yes." I couldn't keep the fear out of my voice.

The woman spoke again, her voice firm and in com-
mand. "Debra, is that you? This is Eve Mallory. It is you,
isn't it, Debra?" The extension slammed down, the hollow
sound vanished.

"Sunny, it must be Debra. You must call the—"

And the phone went dead.

I punched the large square button on the base. "Mrs. Mallory? Mrs. Mallory, are you there?"

No dial tone, no static, just an extremely dead phone line.

After putting the receiver back onto the phone's base, I waited. I knew Jazz-Rhonda-Debra would be in soon. I wondered where Karen was hanging out. Was she another character, or another victim?

The girl appeared at the door. Her jaw was set and her expression ice.

"You couldn't stop, could you? You had to keep going and ruin it for everybody."

I leaned back in the chair. Something told me that exposing fear to this girl would be a fatal mistake.

Propping my head on the back of the chair, I pulled in a long, deep breath and released it. I didn't look toward the doorway or the girl; instead, I let my gaze lift, ever so slowly, to the ceiling. I spoke as if bored, as if everything were obvious.

"You cut the phone wires." It was a statement, not a question.

I still didn't turn my head toward her. I hoped my attitude put the girl off stride.

"I thought the lines were underground or something. I didn't think it was so easy to do," I said.

"That just proves you're not as smart as you think." I was pleased at her lame answer. My cool attitude was unexpected.

I rolled my head to one side, looked at the girl, and smiled. A small smile, rueful but just a bit smug. I saw a shadow flit across the girl's expression. Confusion and, if I was lucky, the first stirring of fear.

"Sit down, Jazz." I laughed. "Or Rhonda or Debra or whoever the hell else you think you are." I pointed to the overstuffed chair across the room. "That one is comfy, but you should know that. You liked to sit there and play word games with Dad. Don't you remember?"

"I don't want to sit, and you're not smart enough to play word games. Why were you talking to that woman?"

"Suit yourself." I rocked back and plopped my feet on the desk. "What woman?"

"The woman on the phone."

"Oh, *that* woman. Why would you cut the phone lines if you didn't know?"

"I . . . I . . . I thought she sounded familiar, but I . . . uh . . ." The girl blinked and the change in persona I witnessed before washed over her. She seemed uncertain, and she glanced around the room as if she had awakened in an unfamiliar place.

I spoke in the soft, gentle tone I used when Mom was

upset. "Debra, that was Mrs. Mallory. You remember her, don't you? Rhonda's mother? I'll bet you miss Rhonda, don't you?"

The girl looked at me, then reached up and held onto the door frame as if she needed support. "They loved her. They would never . . . forget her."

"No, they'd never forget her. Who forgot you, Deb?"

The change was as sudden as a snake's strike.

"Stop!" The girl returned to the present. "You stop it. You're just like the doctors. You'll be sorry for this, Sunny. You should have just let it alone. I came here to make up for all the mean things I did before. I wanted to make it right, but you wouldn't let it alone."

I gaped, letting my confusion show. I tried to cover up and bring back the bored, knowing expression.

"There are a few things we need to discuss. I wish you'd sit down and talk to me, Jazz." I used my sister's name as if I were administering a tranquilizer.

It worked. The girl sank into the leather chair, her fingertips scratching and working the arms.

"I don't know exactly what's going on," I began. "But I want to know."

The girl eyed the room, looking for escape routes, looking for something familiar.

"Why did you come here?"

She stared at the floor, then up at me. All the Jazzness streamed off her. "I wanted to come home."

"But this isn't your home." I said it like I was reporting a fact, but something was building in me. Both of us lived in the shadows of dead girls. Neither of us had a real home.

The girl sighed. "It could have been. All you had to do was let it happen."

I talked loud so whatever was pushing couldn't get all the way into my head. "You can't put on Jazz's clothes and take over Jazz's life and think my parents are going to love you like they did her."

She didn't say anything. She did something worse. Her expression sang pity.

"They can't love you," I said. I shut my eyes and breathed. I spoke with my eyes still closed. If I had to speak it and hear it, I didn't have to see it. "They can't love anybody but Jazz. They never will."

There it was. The wall I'd banged my head against. I wasn't even angry. My parents couldn't help it. They were flawed people. They might have the flesh-and-bone kind of love for a child, but they didn't, couldn't love Sunny. The anger I'd nurtured all my life drained from me, just as the Jazzness had left the girl sitting across from me. The girl who was ruining her life searching for love that belonged to someone else.

"Why did Mrs. Mallory say you were dangerous?"

For a minute, the girl didn't say anything. "It was a little fire in my foster home. It wouldn't have done much. I set it right under the smoke alarm."

"Kind of like slamming a door when you leave the room?"

"Yeah."

I knew how that felt. Take a look at the mailbox. We were silent. I was so tired. "I need to know the truth. Did you set the fire in the apartment? Did you kill my sister?"

It was hard to believe this girl had been taller than Jazz, she looked so small now. "No. I was angry. Jazz had it all. But she was worse than that. She didn't want anyone else to have anything. She took my boyfriend, moved him in, and told me to leave."

She brushed her hand in the air, like I'd seen Mom do. "I already had the rep job in Vermont. I stole Jazz's wallet. It's—something I do. I steal wallets."

I didn't say anything.

"I was going to run up her credit card, but I heard about the fire."

I nodded. "And you wanted more than a shopping spree."

The girl shrugged. "Jazz used to complain about how her parents smothered her. Loved her too much." She locked her gaze on me. "I wanted that. To be loved that fiercely."

I knew.

"So I waited until my contract run was over. And I came here."

A voice boomed from the doorway. "She's telling the truth. At least about the fire. Rhonda Mallory was in Vermont. Hell, she was onstage the night of the fire."

Dad stood there with a file folder in his hand. "And the fire was caused by someone cooking up a batch of crystal meth two floors below. The explosions set off the gas lines in and below the building."

The girl's forehead creased in thought. "Oh, Strike and Weezer. The neo-Nazis on the third floor." She shook her head. "There was always a stink around their place. A chemical smell." She looked at Dad. "They were both brain-dead. I didn't think they were smart enough for chemistry."

"The evidence is pretty conclusive that they weren't," I said.

Dad shot me a vicious look. When would I ever learn? Was I hateful because they didn't love me, or did they not love me because . . . Did it matter?

Dad reached into his pocket and pulled out a cell phone. He stabbed the buttons. "You're a menace. I don't care if you started the fire or not. You ruin lives. You hurt people." He turned his attention to the receiver.

My hand shot out in a knee-jerk reflex and slapped the phone out of his hand. It skittered across the desktop. I snatched it and killed the connection. I held the phone behind me.

"No!" The girl and I spoke together.

"Give me the phone, Sunny. This girl is guilty of lots of things that can put her away. She won't be hurting people anymore."

I trembled, but my voice held steady. "No, Dad. I can't let you do that. I can't even explain it. But I can't send her to jail."

"Sunny, quit being stupid and stubborn."

I ignored him. "Go," I told the girl. "Take the station wagon in the shed. Leave it at the bus station. Stop stealing lives. Go back to your own."

The girl's laugh was sad. "I don't know who that is."

"Sunny!"

"Dan, hush." Mom stood at the doorway. She looked the way Dad had when he realized the girl arriving in the cab was not Jazz. I had never witnessed a sadness so complete. She looked at Not-Jazz for a long, slow minute. Then she turned to Dad and locked eyes with him. Her voice was firm. There would be no arguing with that tone. "Sunny's right. We have to tell her good-bye and let her leave."

"Lily, have you all gone crazy?"

"Mom?"

"Yes, Sunny, I know. I've always known. I'm depressed, not delusional."

The pieces started to come together. "You knew she wasn't Jazz. That's why you didn't call Granny and Grandpa. That's why you didn't want me to tell Ms. Collins," I said.

Mom put her hands over her eyes, pressing. "The Lord gave me a chance to pretend. I was able to hug this girl, and love her, just for a while. I got a chance to say good-bye to Jazz."

Releasing her eyes, she stumbled a bit as she went to the girl. Mom took her into her arms and hugged her. "Good-bye." Mom's eyes were glazed with tears. "Sunny's right. You have to go. I know what it's like to be lost. But you can't find yourself if you keep hiding."

She stepped back. "Go."

And the girl left.

We heard her grab her bag from Jazz's room, we heard her shoes on the stairs, we heard the door slam, and we heard the station wagon leave the shed. She wasn't in a hurry. This girl was used to leaving.

Dad slammed a fist into the wall and sank into the leather chair. "What have you two done?"

Mom and I didn't answer.

———

Later, Dad said we had aided and abetted a criminal. "To protect ourselves, we have to agree on something." He eyed us. "This never happened. We didn't get a letter and no one came here. Nothing. It never happened." He sighed. "It's a good thing Ollie already thinks I'm delusional. I'll tell him that I found out the roommate had nothing to do with the fire, and he won't press it." He looked at Mom and me. "And we never talk about it again. Not to anyone. Not even to each other."

Mom nodded.

Dad left.

I was through trying to be the sane one in this house. My head couldn't take any more run-ins with my parents' brick wall.

I picked up the phone and called the only person I could think of who could sort out this mess. I knew her only from holiday visits. But she was a no-nonsense woman. In one of our infrequent phone calls, she said she had moved to Florida hoping my mother would "take hold of herself" if she didn't have another, stronger person to use as a crutch.

"Granny, it's me, Sunny. I need you."

Granny listened to me. "You'd have been better off if you'd been raised by wolves. I'll be there tomorrow."

She arrived, and her first task was to rip open the closed wooden shutters. It went uphill from there. She listened to my story again. She read the letter and Jazz's journal, and prowled through the stuff on my desk. She talked to Mom. She called Dad and talked to him.

She sent me back to school. She picked me up the last day and drove me straight to a therapist.

Granny and I talked, the therapist and I talked, Mom and Dad talked to the therapist. They didn't talk much to me.

And so the summer went. The Summer of Therapy. Me insisting that Not-Jazz had been here. Mom and Dad insisting she had not. Learning new words like *enabler* and *codependent.* Hearing that I would never be a complete person if I stayed in my home. Learning, as Granny had learned years ago, that my parents would either self-destruct or recover—with or without me.

Granny was helping me pack my new butter-smooth leather luggage in late August. I was on my way to boarding school.

"I hate Florida. All those old men with their skinny white legs and black nylon socks. And your Grandpa loves the place. When he bought a pair of plaid shorts, I thought I'd—"

"Granny, stop!"

She paused in her folding. "Good gracious, child, don't shout at me."

I sat in the rocking chair. "You tell me now. Do you believe me or them?"

Granny's eyes didn't turn away. "Do I think a girl came here pretending to be Jazz?"

I nodded.

"No, Sunny. I don't."

"What about Mrs. Mallory?"

"She didn't actually speak to Jazz, did she?"

And there it was.

I pulled the journal from my desk. The letter was inside.

"Then where did this come from? This is proof."

Granny sat on the bed, smoothed the sweater she had been folding, placed it next to her, and took the journal.

"Sunny, you've been forging Lily's name on school notes since you were ten. You paid the bills this last year, signing your mother's name. My guess is that you can do a passable forgery of Dan's signature, too."

Busted.

"Look at this journal, Sunny. It's more about you than about Jazz. When was Jazz ever concerned about anyone else? She was always the main character in her own play."

I guess my face showed surprise.

"Oh, yes, I loved Jazz, but she was a con artist. A good one." Granny's eyes filled. She cleared her throat.

"But this journal. No, that's not Jazz. These are words you needed. You needed a way to give Jazz back to your parents so you could leave."

"But—"

"Sunny, look at your desk."

The Leonardo book was there. My practice notebook next to it.

"When you do the mirror-writing, is it your own handwriting backwards?"

I looked. "No," I whispered. Afraid now.

"No." Granny's voice was soothing. Like mine when I didn't want to spook Mom. "It's exactly like Leonardo da Vinci's."

She handed me the journal. "You wrote this."

I love my new school. I love not being Jazz Reynolds's sister. I love being a kid, not a fake adult.

My edges are softening. I have friends.

Dad isn't doing well in AA. I think he likes being a drunk. I can't help him with that. Mom is better. Granny will stay until Thanksgiving. Then she's leaving. Mom has to be a grown-up. She's trying. She might even make it.

I still see a therapist.

———————

It was Friday. I had plans with friends for the weekend. I took the wide oak steps two at a time, into the burgundy-carpeted entry hall. I opened my mailbox. Only one letter.

On yellow stationery.

I pulled it out and stared at the address.

"Wow, weird."

The voice came from over my shoulder, making me jump.

"What's weird?"

Kim, my roommate, pointed at the letter. "That's your handwriting. Sending letters to yourself?"

My head roared and my vision tilted. I leaned against the wall for balance and ripped open the letter.

"Took a while to find you. Planning to see you soon."

The signature was spiky and back-slanted.

"Sunny."

What have I done?